"If I'm going to work on this house, you're going to help me…"

"What's up?" Jack asked. "Your face is flushed again."

To prevent him from asking any further questions, Grace stuck out her hand and said, "If I agree to your outrageous terms, do we have a deal?"

What was she saying? She couldn't get out of town fast enough to prevent Jack from somehow discovering the truth she'd hidden from him for twelve long years. Yet here she was agreeing to stay and help. Still, she really needed to have the house restored before it completely fell to pieces.

And besides, how hard could it be watching Jack working under the hot sun? Seeing him again, she couldn't get rid of the notion they had unfinished business.

She'd kept her secret safe this long, she could keep it to herself a bit longer….

Dear Reader,

One of my favorite romance themes is the reunion story. I wonder what it's like to be reunited with your high school or college sweetheart?

In *Sweet Home Colorado*, Jack O'Malley, the last of the O'Malley men to find love, is knocked off his feet when his high school sweetheart, Grace Saunders, returns to Spruce Lake. At first he's reluctant to have anything to do with Grace, but he soon finds himself under her spell and agreeing to renovate the house she's inherited from her great-aunt.

Jack is the one person Grace hopes she won't run into in Spruce Lake, but—doing a bit of matchmaking—her lawyer employs Jack as the contractor responsible for renovating the old Victorian that now belongs to her.

Grace has a secret she's kept from Jack for more than a dozen years, and now her greatest fear is that he'll discover what it is!

Did I tell you my other favorite theme was secret babies?

Find out how Grace and Jack's relationship develops into love and how they resolve their differences once Jack discovers Grace's secret.

This is the fifth and final installment of The O'Malley Men series. I hope you've enjoyed seeing the O'Malley brothers fall in love as much as I have.

I enjoy hearing from readers. You can write to me at cc@cccoburn.com.

Happy reading and healthy lives!

C.C. Coburn

Sweet Home Colorado

C.C. COBURN

H HARLEQUIN® AMERICAN ROMANCE®

Recycling programs
for this product may
not exist in your area.

ISBN-13: 978-0-373-75443-4

SWEET HOME COLORADO

Printed in U.S.A.

ABOUT THE AUTHOR

C.C. Coburn was born in the heart of Australia's outback, then moved to its Pacific Coast. She's traveled the world, lived in England, Austria and the USA and still counts traveling as one of her passions.

She learned to ski in Austria, then discovered Colorado's majestic Rocky Mountains and bought a home there. She now divides her time between Australia, Colorado and England, where one of her three children lives. Her other children still call Australia home.

C.C. shares her life with a beautiful Labrador and a man who, after thirty-two years of marriage, still looks pretty darned good in his kilt.

Books by C.C. Coburn
HARLEQUIN AMERICAN ROMANCE

Many thanks to

My faithful reader Jan Durkin.
Talented author and nurse Fiona Lowe.
Handyman Garth Stroble.
My wonderful editor, Paula Eykelhof.
And as always, Keith.

Prologue

"Jack? Are you still there?"

Jack O'Malley took a seat on the front steps of the house he'd just finished restoring in Spruce Lake, Colorado. He cradled his cell phone against his shoulder and wiped his brow. It was hot. Damned hot for June. Especially June in the Rockies. "I'm still here, Mike, and the answer's still no."

"C'mon, it's only an estimate. You've got time for that, haven't you?"

Jack groaned. It was flattering to be in demand for his services as a contractor who specialized in high-quality home-building and renovation, but one day he'd like to be able to take a holiday. With the way work kept piling up, that wasn't going to happen any time in the next decade. And now his friend and lawyer, Mike Cochrane, wanted to heap on more work. He'd already turned down the same job late last week, when Mike first contacted him about it. Now Mike was sounding desperate.

"Like I told you, Jack, my client's a doctor. And you know how much I need new clients—*wealthy* ones."

Jack gave a snort of disgust. "And like I told *you*, Mike, the answer's still no."

"Aw, c'mon, Jack. *Buddy,*" he said, drawing out the last word. "You're the only person capable of restoring that Victorian on Lincoln."

Just as it had last week, Jack's heart rate kicked up a notch at the mention of the old house. Gracie Saunders, the girl he'd dated in high school, had lived there. Missy Saunders, her great-aunt, had owned the house, but she'd moved to the Twilight Years retirement home a decade ago. The place had been rented out over the years, until it fell into such a state of disrepair no one wanted to live there. Missy had passed away a couple of years back and Jack assumed the house had been sold to the doctor—who'd probably, like too many of Spruce Lake's second-home owners, use it two weeks a year and leave it vacant for the other fifty.

He took a long swig of orange juice. "Since when did you start pimping for clients wanting their houses restored?"

"Since a friend of a friend told this doctor I had contacts here in Spruce Lake. Contacts who were *reliable.*"

Jack didn't miss the inflection in Mike's voice. If he said no to the estimate, he'd be letting Mike down. Mike had done a lot for the O'Malleys, especially helping Jack's brother Will foil the development company that had wanted to tear down half the old buildings on Main Street and put up a bunch of condos and a shopping mall. Their plan would've destroyed the Victorian-era character of the town. Instead, Will and his supporters had saved the buildings from destruction and Jack had spent the past few years restoring many of them.

But his next project was building a new home for Adam, his wife, Carly, and their kids. Adam had got land at a bargain-basement price from Will, who'd recently subdivided the ranch he'd bought a dozen years earlier into ranchettes of around ten acres each. The ranchettes had funded the purchase of buildings on Main Street to save them from destruction.

Jack couldn't disappoint Adam and Carly. The house they presently lived in was getting to be way too small for Adam's growing family. Jack's youngest brother had married a widow with four children. Then they'd adopted two dogs and a cat from the animal shelter. And now Carly was pregnant.

"I'd love to restore that beauty to her former grandeur, Mike, but right now I don't have the time. You know I'm slated to start work on Adam and Carly's place next."

It sure would be nice to renovate the old Victorian, though. The house had stood empty and neglected for too long. Jack scratched the rash on the inside of his elbow, then felt the need to scratch the one behind his knee. He'd have to see a doctor about the damned things pretty soon. *Another* doctor. That senile old fool Jenkins and his expensive creams hadn't helped the rashes he'd been plagued with for the past couple of months. In fact, they just kept getting worse. The guy ought to be put out to pasture. "When's your client going to be here?"

"Tomorrow. And I'm supposed to have found and employed a contractor by then."

"Again, I don't understand why you're so hung up on me doing this. I didn't know lawyers did stuff like that for their clients."

"Jack, lawyers would walk barefoot over hot coals for their clients."

Jack let out a guffaw of derision. "Yeah, right! Pull the other leg—it plays 'Jingle Bells.' What you mean is—so long as they pay you enough, you'd do the hot-coals walk."

"I've already received a hefty advance for finding the right contractor. Naturally, the doc is now one of my most important clients."

"Yeah, he's probably, apart from me, your *only* client!"

He could hear the smile in Mike's voice. One thing Mike wasn't short of was clients. Too bad a lot of them failed to pay up. "C'mon, Jack. Gimme a break and get an estimate to me, ASAP?"

Jack grimaced. He knew what Mike was saying and it wasn't too far from the truth—his lawyer could do with building up his client base. A *paying* client base. Too often softhearted Mike ended up footing the bill for his clients. Snaring a doctor, one prepared to send an advance, was a coup.

Spruce Lake, nestled in the Colorado Rockies, was a ski and summer resort that, until a decade ago, had been a well-kept secret. However, it was now being discovered, and those in the know had been snapping up properties for a good few years. That helped boost the local economy, but Jack wasn't sure he welcomed the change to his formerly sleepy hometown.

In Jack's opinion, Spruce Lake was picture-postcard perfect. Filled with a mixture of old Victorians and more modern homes, its main attraction was an unsurpassed ski mountain during the winter. It also offered myriad summer activities from hiking and bike riding to golfing and white-water rafting, fishing, mine tours and a thriving Main Street market.

The only problem, according to the Chamber of Commerce, was that the rest of the world had barely heard of the place. Sure, Aspen and Vail were household names for the dedicated skier, celebrity and socialite, but Spruce Lake had yet to be discovered by the glitterati—which suited Jack just fine. Small-town life was what he knew and loved. He didn't want to live anywhere else, and if this rich doctor client of Mike's wanted to preserve some of the town's unique beauty by restoring Missy Saunders's old Victorian, then he should be willing to help out—a little, anyway.

"I'll see what I can do about an estimate, Mike."

"Great! I knew I could rely on you, buddy. Can I have it first thing tomorrow?"

"You're kidding, right?"

"No, I'm serious. This is urgent."

Jack sighed. Mike was certainly keen to impress his client. "You seem to forget there's more than the carpentry to quote on. There's also, plumbing, electrical, roofing—"

"Yeah, yeah. A guesstimate will be fine. I just need something!"

Jack shook his head. Mike wasn't going to quit nagging until he agreed. "I'll get it to you by noon. How's that sound? And listen, it's just an estimate for comparison purposes. I really don't have the time to do the work. I've made a promise to Adam and Carly."

"Yeah, yeah. Listen, I gotta go." He suddenly cut the connection.

Jack stared at his cell phone. For someone who

claimed he didn't have enough paying clients, Mike sure was busy. Since moving back to town from a big practice in Colorado Springs, the guy had gotten himself elected to the Chamber of Commerce, so maybe he had some business to attend to there.

He wasn't due anywhere for a couple of hours so Jack figured he might as well head over to the house. He wouldn't need a key to get in—one of the front windows had been smashed recently by some kids on spring break. At the very least, he should board it up against further vandalism.

Chapter One

Jack eased his old truck against the curb behind a bright red BMW Z4 parked outside Missy Saunders's and wished he had the time to work on the house. He hated to see the magnificent old buildings of the former gold-mining town lying unloved and unkept. This home was a particularly fine specimen, built by a miner who'd struck it rich with a huge nugget back in the 1870s. It had passed down through the miner's family, eventually going to Missy Saunders. Missy was an only child and had never married. Jack guessed it had been sold long ago to pay Missy's nursing-home fees. The sweet old lady had spent a while at the Twilight Years before passing on. Jack regretted he hadn't been living in Spruce Lake so he could've attended her funeral—especially since his mom had reported that Gracie had made a brief appearance to pay her respects to her great-aunt. He wished he'd seen her then. It might have helped him make up his mind about a few things, maybe get her out of his system once and for all.

He shook his head to clear it. No point in reminiscing about what might have been. He and Gracie were history. She was never coming back to town; she'd told him as much. He really needed to get over her and move on with his life. His realization that he was still in love with her had helped him decide that he'd never make a priest and he'd left the seminary in L.A. before being ordained. Although there'd been other reasons for leaving, Gracie had been the main one. But she was a married woman and therefore off-limits, so instead he'd channeled his energies into a carpentry apprenticeship, then worked with underprivileged kids helping them learn a trade and life skills. It was rewarding work, but a lonely life nevertheless.

Since returning to Spruce Lake a couple of years ago, Jack had restored many of the town's Victorian-era buildings—but none of them had the size and grandeur of Missy Saunders's place. Still, there were other contractors in the county, whom Mike had probably been sweet-talking all week. Funny that no one else had taken on the project.

Parked in front of the sports car was his new truck, emblazoned with *Jack O'Malley Constructions* on the doors. Jack had taken delivery of the Dodge Ram only last week. And he hated it. It was just too new and shiny for him. He preferred his old Ford F150.

Jack had had Betsy since high school and, before that, she'd been used to run around the family ranch, Two Elk. She had over a million miles on the clock and wasn't missing a beat. Her seats were worn and comfortable and fitted Jack's butt like a glove.

He'd felt like a traitor when he'd taken Betsy down to trade her in on the Dodge. They'd offered peanuts for her, so he'd kept Betsy *and* bought the Dodge.

Two days later he gave the Dodge to his foreman, Al Hernandez, to drive. Al was only too happy to use the boss's truck, with its smell of new leather and its too shiny paintwork. Al had three young boys, and the twin cab arrangement suited his family perfectly.

Jack had arranged to meet Al at the house, figuring the two of them would get through the assessment twice as fast. He'd blow this doctor off with a ridiculously high estimate and then he'd be able to start on Adam's place with a clear conscience—and the knowledge that another contractor in town would get the job. Not that any other contractor would be as good as Jack and his team, but what did this doctor think? That he could snap his fingers and have someone start immediately?

The door of the sports car opened and a woman stepped out. Her dark hair fell across her face, hiding her features, but Jack didn't miss the oh-so-long legs and trim figure as she stalked around the front of her sports car and onto the sidewalk.

She walked with confidence, like a woman used to getting her own way. She, and the car, looked totally out of place in Spruce Lake. Jack's hometown was more battered SUVs, jeans and cowboy boots—not flashy sports cars, designer dresses and six-inch heels.

One of those heels wedged itself in a crack in the sidewalk.

Jack watched as she bent to pull it out, revealing a lot more leg…and the bright red undersides of her shoes.

He enjoyed the show, wondering who this fish out of water could be visiting in Spruce Lake, because for sure she wasn't local. Jack would've noticed her way before this if she was.

He could hear her cursing through the open window of his truck. *Time to rescue the damsel in distress,* he decided as he climbed out and sauntered over to the woman. "Need any help?" he asked.

She stopped cussing and pulling at her leg long enough to stand up to her full height and look him in the eye.

Jack felt the sucker punch right to his gut. He'd know those bewitching light brown eyes, that pert nose, those soft full lips, anywhere.

Gracie.

She'd lost a good fifteen pounds, had her hair cut and styled and was wearing way too much makeup, but it was her, all right.

He swallowed and said, "Hi, Gracie."

She frowned and said, "Do I know you?"

Jack felt the sucker punch again as she reminded him how insignificant a part of her life he'd been, in spite of their dating for nearly two years in high school.

He pulled off his sunglasses and held out his hand. "Jack O'Malley. We dated for a while. Remember?"

Jack had fallen hard for Gracie the day she'd entered his classroom in their junior year. She'd graduated with an A-plus average, while Jack—thanks to his dyslexia— had barely scraped through. She'd won a scholarship to college, then medical school. Jack hadn't fared quite so well—at least, not scholastically. He'd joined the peace corps right out of high school and worked on projects around the world for two years. He'd come home, drifted through college. Then, believing it was the best way to answer his calling to help others, he entered the seminary.

She stared at Jack, glanced at Betsy and then at his shiny new truck with *Jack O'Malley Constructions* on the door, and finally back at him. "Jack? *You're* my contractor?"

"You inherited the house from your Aunt Missy?"

She shrugged. "Sort of. It's a long story."

One Jack was curious about since if anyone should have inherited, he'd expected it to be Gracie's bum of a father. So Mike was well aware of who the owner was and Jack's connection to her.

Meddling Mike wasn't above a bit of matchmaking. Well, he'd lose any bets on this one.

Mike probably figured Jack wouldn't be able to say no to his high school sweetheart. Mike was wrong.

"I'm not your contractor," he said, almost wishing—perversely—that he was. He had something to prove to Gracie Saunders. "I agreed to do an estimate, for comparison's sake. That's all."

"He told me…" She suddenly seemed to remember that her shoe was still stuck in the sidewalk and bent again to try pulling it out. Since the heels were so high and her dress so short and tight-fitting, it wasn't an easy task.

"Allow me," Jack said, and knelt at her feet. He grimaced at the metaphor. He'd virtually worshipped the ground Gracie walked on in high school. She'd been his first girlfriend. His first lover. And then she'd walked all over his heart.

He gently grasped her ankle in one hand and her shoe in the other.

GRACE FELT A SHOT of heat race up her leg at Jack's touch. She watched as those big, capable hands eased her foot from her Christian Louboutin pump and placed it on the sidewalk while he worked on getting her shoe out of the crack. Jack had sure grown up. No wonder she hadn't recognized him. He was so much taller, so much broader. Jack was no longer a high school boy; he was a man, and that resonated deep inside her.

But Jack was the one person whose path she hadn't wanted to cross in Spruce Lake. If they spent any time together, she was afraid he'd discover her secret, which had the potential to destroy them both.

"Careful!" she warned as he pulled her shoe from the walk.

Jack stood to his full height, towering over her by at least eight inches now that she was balancing on her foot without the benefit of six-inch heels.

He examined the shoe, then handed it to her, saying, "Why anyone would want to wear something as impractical as this is beyond my comprehension."

Grace had worn those shoes to impress. Impress anyone from her past she might happen to run into in Spruce Lake. She wanted to show them that Grace Saunders—in spite of her crappy home life, her loser parents, her hand-me-down clothes—had made good. In fact, she'd made better than good. She was a successful Boston pediatrician with a long list of patients.

Her shoulders sagged. A list of patients she'd handed over in her haste to leave town. She might be financially secure and successful. But she was also completely burned out.

She took the shoe from Jack and examined the heel. It was shattered. She cursed.

"*Thank you* is the usual form of appreciation in this town," he said.

She glanced up at him and said, "So, I heard you'd become a priest or something?"

HE NODDED. "OR SOMETHING. I'm now a contractor." No point in telling her the whole story. She wouldn't be in town long enough for it to matter.

"*My* contractor."

He shook his head. "I've already told Mike I couldn't do this job."

"Even if I paid you double?"

Now he stuck both hands in the back pockets of his jeans. She had him there. Money always talked and he had plenty of community projects he could direct some extra funds to, but Adam and Carly were family. He owed them.

"Not even then."

"I don't remember you being such a hard case in high school, Jack," she said, practically batting her eyelashes at him.

"High school was a long time ago, Gracie," he said, since she seemed to be avoiding the fact that they'd dated for two years.

When Gracie had put her name forward as a peer tutor, Jack, struggling because of dyslexia, had signed up. They'd spent a lot of time together after school hours and eventually he'd built up the courage to ask her out. She'd said, "What took you so long? Where did you have in mind?"

Jack had been so flabbergasted, never believing she'd say yes, that he didn't have anywhere in mind. Except to go parking at Inspiration Point, the local necking spot.

Not that he'd ever necked with a girl. And he didn't get to do it that night, either. But later...

"What do you mean, 'Not even then'?" she demanded, bringing him back to the present.

Jack crossed his arms and widened his stance. "I'm due to start work on my brother's house outside town tomorrow. I don't break my promises."

GRACE ADMIRED HIS candor. Then a need to prick the confidence he was projecting made her say, "Didn't you break your promise to the church by leaving the priesthood?" Aunt Missy had written her about it.

His eyes narrowed. "My relationship with the church, and why I left, is none of your business."

Dammit! She was intrigued and couldn't let it go. "Did you fall in love with one of your parishioners?"

"And you just stepped way over the mark." He gave her a tiny salute, saying, "Goodbye, Gracie," turned on his heel and headed to his truck. "I'd say it's been a pleasure. But it hasn't."

"It's Grace!" she shouted to his back. "Not *Gracie.*" How dare he just walk away like that!

He shrugged and pulled open the door of his truck. "Whatever," he said, and climbed in.

"Wait!" she cried, and hobbled toward his truck, one shoe on and one off.

She went to rest her arms on the passenger's side window frame, then noticed it was dusty. She touched the frame with her fingertips and leaned in. "I'm sorry, Jack. I didn't mean to pry."

"Yes, you did." He started the truck.

"You can't leave me here like this! You promised to give me an estimate."

"I promised Mike I'd give him an estimate. That was before I knew who his doctor client was. Goodbye, Grace."

Chapter Two

Jack hated being played for a sucker. Mike knew exactly who he was dealing with, that was why he'd avoided using the doctor's name. And Mike knew that Jack wouldn't want to have anything to do with Grace. She'd left town, and him, without a backward glance after winning a full scholarship to a college in Boston faster than a snowflake melted in July. For too many years he'd tried to forget her. Now here she was, back in Spruce Lake and acting as if there'd been nothing between them.

And why shouldn't she? She'd moved on, married, probably had kids. It cut deep that she hadn't recognized him right away. He'd obviously spent too much time loving someone who didn't feel the same way about him.

It hadn't helped that during his time in the peace corps he'd been posted to remote places, often without internet access. They'd exchanged letters for a while, but Grace was always slow to respond, and when she did, it was all about college, the people she was hanging out with, how much she loved life in Boston.

Jack eventually realized she was letting him down as nicely as she could. He later heard she'd graduated from college early and gone to medical school. Then she'd married. Lost, Jack had entered the seminary, believing he could help others. He'd wasted too many years dreaming of Grace. Now that she was here in the flesh, he had no intention of letting her under his skin again.

He put Betsy in gear, ready to get out of there—make a symbolic break with Grace. He glanced at her manicured fingertips still resting on Betsy's window frame, hoping she'd take the hint and move.

"Mike didn't tell you it was me who wanted the estimate?" she said, her voice barely above a whisper.

Her frown and confused tone had him cursing under his breath. He turned off the ignition and scratched the inside of his elbow.

"I wonder why not," she said, a little too loudly now that Betsy's engine was no longer thumping away.

Jack wasn't going to tell her why not. Mike knew that if Jack had any idea who the client was, he'd have refused outright. He wanted to hit himself upside the head for not making the connection. Mike sure had suckered him. He'd suckered Grace, too. He scratched the back of his neck.

Suddenly Grace was climbing into the passenger seat. An erotic fantasy—involving him and Grace in Betsy's cab—filled Jack's mind as she ran her hand down the inside of his elbow. Then she leaned in close to look at the back of his neck before he could react and tell her to get the hell out of his truck.

"Whoa! What are you doing?" he demanded, pulling away from her, worried his fantasy might come true. Half-worried it might not.

"Taking a look at your arm. And your neck."

Jack edged farther away from her, embarrassed about the rashes.

"What if we make a deal?" she said.

"About?"

"If I cure you of these rashes, will you do the renovation for me?"

Much as Jack wanted to be done with the rashes and all the scratching, he had a prior obligation to his brother. "Nope," he said, and resisted the urge to scratch the back of his knee. He felt as if he was carrying a contagious disease and wondered why Grace was even sitting in the truck with him. Apparently she wasn't afraid of catching it.

She jumped as Al stuck his head through the passenger window. Al had the stocky build of his Mexican father and the height of his English-born mother. But Jack doubted it was Al's physique that had Grace scooting across the seat. It was more likely the snake tattoo that ran from Al's right wrist up his arm, disappeared into the sleeve of his T-shirt and emerged to coil around his throat. Several times. Grace couldn't take her eyes off it.

"Hey, boss," he said to Jack, and nodded to Grace.

Jack's cell rang. He retrieved it from his pocket and saw that the call was from Adam. If it had been from Mike, he would've ignored it.

"Hey, Adam. What can I do for you?"

"You know how you're supposed to start work on our house?"

"Ye-es," Jack said slowly, suspicion creeping up his spine.

"Well, I'm wondering if you have anything else you

could do instead. Carly wants to stay closer to the hospital until after the baby arrives. She has short labors and she's worried the extra distance from the new house will mean the difference between giving birth in the hospital and giving birth in the car. To tell you the truth, I'd prefer the first option."

This had Mike's meddling written all over it. "I thought you were spilling out of the house on Washington?"

"We are. But that bothers me a lot less than not making it to the hospital in time."

"So you want me to delay starting your renovation?"

"If you could."

The tentacles of suspicion crept further up Jack's spine. "Has Mike called you today?"

"Mike who?"

Jack's lips thinned. So now it was a conspiracy involving Mike *and* Adam to throw him and Grace together for the summer. He glanced at Grace. She looked completely innocent.

"I'll get back to you," he said, and shut off his phone.

"Grace, this is my foreman, Al Hernandez."

She offered her hand and Al shook it vigorously.

"I've been waiting for you at the back of the house, boss," Al said. "Yet I find you here, making time with the prettiest *señorita* this side of the Front Range."

Jack climbed out of the truck while Al stood back and opened the door for Grace. She slipped past him with a whispered "Thank you" and hobbled to her vehicle. Jack enjoyed the view as she bent to remove her other shoe, opened the trunk and fished around inside it. She straightened, dropped a pair of fancy flip-flops on the ground and stepped into them.

"That's better," she said, coming over to them. "I'm Grace Saunders, by the way." She flashed Al a smile and Jack could see his burly foreman melting under her charms.

Jack cleared his throat. "Shouldn't you be getting home to Maria *and the children?*" For some stupid reason he needed to let Grace know that Al was spoken for, even though he was the one who'd prevented Al from getting home by asking to meet him here.

"Just as soon as we've done this estimate, boss."

The three of them headed toward the house, going in through the squeaky front gate and up the weed-covered path. Al continued to the back of the house, saying, "I'll finish measuring up the outside. Do you have a key?"

"Nope." Jack reached inside the smashed pane of one of the front windows, releasing the catch. He pulled up the window and hoisted himself inside. Before he could open the front door, Grace followed him in, climbing over the sill.

MEMORIES FLOODED GRACE—memories she wasn't prepared for. She staggered and Jack caught her arm.

"I *was* going to open the door for you," he said.

Grace wasn't going to correct his misunderstanding that climbing through the window had caused her to lose her balance.

"You're whiter than a ghost," he said. "Would you like to sit down?" Without waiting for an answer, he led her to the stairs.

She sank gratefully onto the first step and forced

herself to smile up at him. "I'm just tired. My body's two hours ahead of my brain and the altitude is bothering me."

"Is there anyone I can call for you? Your husband?"

Grace shook her head. "My...*ex*-husband is back in Boston."

"You're divorced?"

"I certainly hope so. Otherwise, Edward could end up in a lot of trouble with the law. He's planning on getting married again come September. To his first ex-wife."

Jack's grin lit up his face. He'd always had a great smile.

"I heard your half of the conversation with your brother. Since he doesn't need you, what do I have to do to sweet-talk you into restoring this place for me?"

What was she saying? Only a moment ago she was dreading spending any time with Jack for fear he'd discover her secret and now she was practically begging him to take the job!

Jack scratched the inside of his elbow again.

"That offer of a cure is still open, if it'll clinch the deal."

Jack's eyes narrowed. "What are you really doing here, Gracie?"

"Grace," she corrected. "I want this house restored."

"And then what?"

"And then what, what?"

"Stop talking in riddles. Are you going to stay—or are you heading back to Boston?"

"You mean now?"

"Yes. Now. And then when the place is restored, are you flipping it, never to return to Spruce Lake?"

"My life is in Boston." No way was she staying in this backwater where everyone knew everyone else's business and the sidewalks were a death trap for expensive shoes. If Jack took the job, she wouldn't have to hang around Spruce Lake supervising. She could get out of there, away from Jack, away from any fear that he'd discover her secret.

"Then I suggest you go back there. I'll help you find another contractor who won't mind putting his heart and soul into restoring a place only to have it sold off."

"I'm not selling it, Jack. It has to stay in the family. That's a promise I made to Aunt Missy."

Before he could respond, she said, "I'm going to travel around Europe for the next couple of months." She wondered where that had come from. In truth, Grace hadn't given much thought to anything the past couple of days, not since little Cassie Greenfield died.

Her patient's death—one of too many—had been the catalyst for Grace's decision to throw everything in, get away from Boston and dying children and an ex-husband about to remarry and all the people who wanted to remind her of that while trying to set her up with their cousin, or brother or—heaven forbid—their uncle!

Just because Edward had been more than twice her age didn't mean she was looking for *another* older man. It didn't mean she was looking for another man, period! Edward had been a far from satisfactory husband or lover. But she'd married him in her first year of med school, when he was already a well-respected neurosurgeon. She'd craved the respect and financial security marrying Edward would bring. She'd basked in his compliments and ignored the thirty-year age gap—the age gap that meant he didn't want any more children. He had two daughters and a son by his previous wife. They were all horrible to Grace—as was his ex-wife—whenever they happened to cross paths at social functions.

When Cassie Greenfield, a little girl who'd fought so hard and so bravely—like so many of her patients did against cancer—had died, something had died inside Grace. Cassie was the same age her daughter, Amelia, would be now. Her and Jack's daughter.

The guilt she felt at having given up a healthy child, and the cumulative effect of treating so many who weren't healthy, had come to a head that day.

Grace's love of medicine and her belief in herself, that she could cure all the hurt and pain in the world, were shattered. She'd needed to get away, regroup, maybe think about another medical specialty. One that didn't involve dying children.

There was a good reason she'd chosen to specialize in pediatrics—to atone for her sins. The guilt of giving her baby away bit deep. But the real sin she'd committed twelve years earlier was in not telling Jack—of not giving him a chance. That was the one she really needed to answer for. How she could even start to do that, Grace had no idea.

Jack scratched his elbow again. She knew that what he was suffering from was something she could easily cure. With no chance of Jack dying.

"What do you want from me, Jack?" she asked.

His eyebrows rose speculatively.

"Apart from that."

He held up his hands in a gesture of surrender. "Did I say anything?"

She grinned. *That* would doubtless be very nice. She wondered what it would be like to have a young, virile man like Jack make love to her. Instead of a selfish older man like Edward who was also a lousy lover.

Wondering what sort of lover Jack would be, now that he was a man—not a fumbling teen—Grace felt her face heat.

"Are you okay?" Jack asked. "You look flushed."

"I'm fine," she said, working to recover her equilibrium. "But can we negotiate? I'd very much like you to restore this house for me."

"Then you'll have to help with it," he said, and glanced pointedly at her manicured nails.

"You've got to be joking! You have a foreman, so I assume you have a crew of workers. How would I be able to help?"

"You can sweep up, run down to the hardware store for supplies. Make lunch for the gang. Paint walls. Stuff like that."

"And my trip to Europe?"

"You and I both know you just made that up."

Grace chewed her lip. Jack was pretty shrewd. "I'd *like* to go to Europe sometime."

"Then you can. When we've finished this project."

We. The word scared her, especially in relation to Jack. They'd dated for two years but had only made love once—the night before Jack headed off for the peace corps and she left for college. Jack had excited her far more that fateful night than Edward ever did the entire time they were married.

And Jack had given her what Edward never could. Why they'd waited so long to make love, she had no idea. But six weeks later, feeling as if she had a bad case of the flu but suspecting worse in spite of their use of birth control, Grace had purchased a pregnancy test.

When it came back positive, Grace knew she had only two options. Since the first went against her beliefs about preserving human life, she started making inquiries about adoption. If she'd known Jack was in town, Grace would never have come back to Spruce Lake. Her fear that he would discover her secret was too great. She was sure her guilt was written all over her face.

"What's up?" he asked. "Your face is flushed again."

To prevent Jack from asking any further questions she stuck out her hand. "If I agree to your outrageous terms, do we have a deal?"

What was she saying? She couldn't get out of town fast enough to prevent Jack from somehow discovering the truth, yet here she was agreeing to stay and help. Then again, it wasn't like she had anything else to do for the next few months—so why not stay? She owed him that for making time in his schedule and she really needed to have the house restored before it completely fell to pieces. She couldn't live with that sort of disgrace.

And besides, how hard could it be watching Jack working under the hot sun? Seeing him again, she couldn't get rid of the notion they had unfinished business. Business that had nothing to do with the child they shared, but a whole lot to do with sex.

She'd kept her secret safe this long. She could keep it to herself a bit longer.

Jack took her hand and held it. "Deal."

His hand felt warm and strong. Grace didn't want to let it go. Where was Jack when she'd broken down at the hospital the other day? She was sure if she'd had his strong shoulders to lean on, she wouldn't have had such a public meltdown.

Chapter Three

"Boss!"

They jumped apart at Al's shout.

"I'm done with the estimate for the outside. I'll leave the rest to you, okay?" he said. "Maria's giving me hell about getting home for dinner with the kids tonight."

"Sure, sure," Jack said. "Stop by Mrs. Carmichael's and pick up a big bunch of flowers for that wonderful wife of yours." Jack drew his cell out of his pocket. "I'll call Mrs. C. She'll be waiting outside her shop."

Al's face broke into a wide smile. "I knew there was a reason I worked for a slave driver like you!" He saluted Grace. "Bye, ma'am." A moment later he disappeared through the front door.

Grace listened while Jack called the florist. He seemed to be close to her since he could order flowers over the phone without credit card details. *And* have the woman waiting outside her shop to hand Al a bouquet as he drove by!

Jack hung up and said, "Now, how are you going to cure me of this itching? And please don't say it's bedbugs!"

GRACE LAUGHED. JACK LOVED the sound of it, deep-throated and sexy as hell. He'd been a hormonal teen when he'd first laid eyes on Grace in his English class fifteen years ago. He fell for her hard. After they started dating, he'd assumed they'd eventually marry, stay in Spruce Lake, have kids. He made a face at the memory of his teenage delusion.

Turned out she'd had other plans, ones that didn't include him in her future.

During his time in the seminary, he'd worked hard to suppress his memories of her, his desire to hold her and make love to her again.

Grace touched his arm and he reveled in the warmth and silkiness of her fingertips on his skin.

"If I suspected you were suffering from bedbugs, trust me, I'd have hightailed it back to Boston."

He tried to smile, but the thought that Grace might leave again filled him with dread.

"You have eczema." Her voice became serious as she examined the angry red rash. Her hands felt warm on him. Too warm. Too good. "It's not contagious and it's easily curable. Do you suffer from allergies?"

"None that I know of. Why?"

"Because it's often due to an allergic reaction, either to grasses or something you've been eating. Stress can set it off, too. Does asthma run in the family?"

"Mom has it, but nothing severe."

"Uh-huh. Do you drink acidic juices, like orange, pineapple, stuff like that?"

"Not usually, but lately I've been swigging OJ as a pick-me-up."

She nodded. "That's about the worst thing you can

do. I'll make a list of foods to avoid and write you a prescription for a medicated cream. That should take care of it."

"How can a Massachusetts doctor write me a prescription?"

"I took the precaution of getting licensed to practice in Colorado a couple of years ago, in case Aunt Missy was ever moves to a care home in Denver and needed me around for a while."

He considered this, then said, "Doc Jenkins has given me creams before."

"Probably not the right ones. Has he ever talked to you about your diet?"

Jack shook his head, tongue-tied because Grace was absentmindedly stroking the inside of his arm. Didn't she know what it was doing to him?

"Doesn't sound like much of a doctor to me."

"You got that right. He should've retired years ago, but he's the only family doc in town, so we're stuck with him."

"You mean to tell me, after all the years I've been away, there's still only one doctor in Spruce Lake?"

Not wanting to imply that the town only attracted worn-out old coots like Doc Jenkins, he said, "There's a couple of orthopedic guys who come for the winter. They do very well out of all the skiers and snowboarders who break their bones."

"And if a woman would prefer to see a female doctor?"

"Then she has to go to Silver Springs."

"Which, in spite of its proximity to Spruce Lake, is an inconvenience."

"You could always set up practice here," Jack suggested.

"I'm a pediatrician," she said. "Not an OB/GYN." Grace wandered into the kitchen and turned back to him. "If you want to do your estimate, I can swing by the pharmacy and get your cream."

"Sounds good. But first you'd better tell me what you want done with the place."

"We'll get to that in a moment, but since you're insisting I stay in town, I'd like to live here while you do the renovations."

"Hoo, boy."

"You seem to think that's a bad idea."

"Do you realize how much dust'll be involved?"

"No."

"That was a rhetorical question. Trust me, you'd be better off renting somewhere during the reno."

"Since I won't be earning an income while the renovations are going on, I don't want to waste money on rent."

"Yet you were about to embark on an expensive trip through Europe for a couple of months?"

"I seem to remember foolishly offering to pay you double your estimate to get the work done," she said with a shrug.

Jack grinned. "Yeah, there is that."

Grace flashed him one of her brilliant smiles and he said, "I wasn't going to take you up on that, so go find somewhere else to live. People post ads at the super-market all the time."

"Great idea."

"So how is it you came to inherit the house and not your father?" he ventured.

"I didn't inherit it—I bought it from Aunt Missy years ago. You might remember we lived here rent-free in exchange for my dad taking care of the place." She grimaced and Jack understood what Grace meant by it. The house could've been better looked after. Things had come to a head—there'd been accusations of money going missing and Grace's parents had moved on. Grace had stayed to finish high school.

"I was the only person in the family who kept in touch with her. A couple of years after I graduated from med school she wrote and offered me a deal—I buy the house at a reduced rate and she could then afford to move into the Twilight Years. She wanted the house kept in the family. Aunt Missy knew full well that if she willed it to my father, he'd sell it and fritter the money away, so she came up with a plan. Since she was asset-rich but didn't have a lot of savings after my parents fleeced her, and I'd started working and had enough for a down payment, I took out a mortgage and bought the place from Aunt Missy. It was a pretty sneaky way of keeping my father's hands off both the house and the profit he'd make by selling it, but it's what Missy wanted and I was happy to help her out. Aunt Missy moved into the Twilight Years and I rented out the house to help with the mortgage payments. When Missy died, my father flipped out because there was nothing for him in her will and he tried to get me to sign the house over to him. Forget it!"

Jack said, "You and Aunt Missy were sure cut from the same cloth. Smart as whips. And your relationship with your parents?"

"Not good. Not that it ever was. I worked hard to win that scholarship to a college so far away partly because I wanted to get away from them."

IMMEDIATELY AFTER SHE'D said it, Grace wanted to take the words back. Jack would think she wanted to get away from him, too. But that was far from the truth.

She wished, for one fleeting moment, that when she'd discovered she was pregnant with Jack's baby, they could have married, kept their child. But after weighing the pros and cons, she'd decided that if they followed that path, there was no way she'd be able to stay in college and keep up her grades. They'd have struggled financially for the rest of their lives. Grace had been there, done that with her parents and she had no intention of repeating their mistakes.

Her lip curled as she thought, *Yet here you are, a dozen years later, with a rewarding career, a lot of money and no one to love. That's some definition of success.*

"I'm sorry your relationship never resolved itself, Grace. I couldn't imagine not being part of a close family," he said. "I love everyone in my family. And I love that all my brothers are married now and have wives and children. It's the cycle of life."

Grace smiled. "That is such a nice compliment to them. They're very lucky to have someone like you in their lives." *If only I had someone who truly cared about me.*

HER HEARTFELT WORDS filled Jack with warmth. He was about to ask her more about her family when Grace turned and headed toward the stairs.

"Now, what needs to be done up here?" she asked, heading to the second floor.

Jack caught her seconds before she put her foot though a broken board. "For a start, I replace some of these treads. I'll show you which ones to avoid."

"I'm impressed you can pick them out. They all look the same to me."

Ignoring her compliment, he said, "I can put through an order for some oak tomorrow."

Grace smiled. "You can really start that soon?"

"Provided you're happy with my estimate, I can start on this first thing in the morning. At least make it safe to climb the stairs without breaking your neck."

Grace frowned and said, "I guess I should talk about stress management. I don't want you to work so hard you'll end up feeling too stressed to finish the job."

Deep in his heart, Jack knew he couldn't walk out on Grace, couldn't leave her and this magnificent house in the hands of another contractor. "Don't worry about it," he said. "It'll be an honor to work on a place like this."

They took the last step onto the top landing. "Keep away from the railing. It's loose," he warned before they made their way toward the master bedroom.

GRACE STEPPED INTO her parents' old bedroom but wasn't prepared for the memories that assailed her. Aunt Missy had given up her beautiful bedroom with the view of the town for Grace's parents to use. And they'd rewarded her by duping her out of her money. She turned away.

"You'll want to talk to an interior designer," he suggested.

"You don't do that yourself?"

He shook his head. "No, I only perform miracles on the house itself. I know how I'd decorate, but I recommend consulting a professional."

Grace nodded, impressed with Jack's professionalism and attention to detail as she watched him make notes in a booklet.

"Now, the roof," he said. "The insulation—what's left of it—should be replaced. And although the slates seem to be in pretty good condition, I noticed stains on the ceiling, which means water's getting in. I'll have a roofing contractor take a look."

He made another note in the booklet, tore out the page and handed it to her. "This is the number of an interior designer I've worked with before. Get her out here as soon as you can. Feel free to use my name if you have to."

Grace took the proffered paper. "I'll see if she can meet me here tomorrow morning."

"That might be pushing it, but I'll mark the loose steps as we go out, in case she comes when I'm not here."

"Thank you. That's very thoughtful." She followed him down the hallway and paused at the top of the stairs while Jack bent and marked each unsafe step with a piece of chalk.

"Careful," he cautioned as he reached to take her hand. "It's darker than when we came in. I'll get the power connected tomorrow."

He glanced at his watch. "How about if you go to the pharmacy while I finish measuring?"

"I'm on my way."

GRACE RETURNED TO the house thirty minutes later. Jack was sitting on the front porch, once more scribbling in his notebook. The way he bent his head, the book resting on his forearm, brought back memories of him at school, struggling to read a passage in class.

She knew he hated having to read out loud or do oral presentations. Some of the kids had laughed at him when he stumbled over the words. She'd guessed he was dyslexic and felt some of his pain. Grace knew what it was like to be different. She'd hush the other kids, turning to glare at them, surprised when they'd complied. After that, she'd volunteered for peer tutoring.

Jack got up and walked over to meet her as she climbed out of her rental. She handed him the pharmacy bag, saying, "The instructions for use are on the package. Stop the orange juice and I'll check your progress in the morning."

Jack pulled out his wallet, but she stopped him. "It's on me. Consider it gratitude for agreeing to this project on such short notice."

Jack glanced at his watch again, leaving Grace with the uncomfortable feeling that he had better things to do than spend time with her. "I've got a dinner engagement, so I should go," he said. "If there's nothing more you need to discuss tonight, I'll head out."

Sorry he had a date and miffed that he hadn't asked her out instead—although why should he, given their history?—Grace shuddered at the sense of melancholy she felt. She hated this time of day between dusk and dark. She didn't like being alone then.

After the divorce, the friends she thought she could count on were more faithful to Edward than to her. Understandable since most of them had been his friends first. He'd kept her so isolated, she'd had little chance to cultivate true friendships for herself. She knew no one outside the medical world apart from her hairdresser and Pilates instructor. *How pathetic is that?* she thought.

"You okay?" he asked, his eyes reflecting his concern.

Grace forced a smile. "Just tired. It's been a hell of a week. I need to check into my hotel in Silver Springs, take a long, hot shower and crawl into bed."

"I'll get that window repaired and new locks put on all the doors tomorrow, too."

"Thank you for agreeing to renovate this house, Jack," she said. "I really appreciate that you made room for me in your schedule."

"I aim to please." He began to walk to his truck, then paused and turned back. "If you don't have any plans, would you like to come to dinner at the ranch tonight? Mom won't mind another mouth to feed. I'm sure my folks would love to see you."

Taken aback by the unexpected invitation, and the implication that there was neither wife nor girlfriend in the picture, Grace could only stumble over her words.

"Er, no, not tonight, Jack, thanks." She covered an exaggerated yawn. "As I said, I've got some sleep to catch up on, and calls to make." She held up the slip of paper he'd given her.

"See you tomorrow, then," he said. "And don't forget, come dressed to work, not to party."

He gave Grace a long look that took in her too-short dress and left those welcome tingles racing up and down her spine.

"DUMB, JACK, DUMB!" He hit the wheel and berated himself as he drove down Lincoln and turned onto Main. What was he thinking, inviting Grace to dinner with the family? Now she'd know there wasn't a girlfriend in the picture. He almost wished he *did* have a significant other in his life, just to show Grace he'd moved on, forgotten about her. But that would be a complete lie.

He wondered what had really brought her back to Spruce Lake, since she'd made her career such an important part of her life. So important that she'd left Spruce Lake—and him—without a backward glance.

But most of all, he wondered why she was no longer married.

Chapter Four

When Jack arrived at Two Elk, the family ranch, that evening, the front yard was already crowded with his brothers' vehicles.

The babies and toddlers would all be tucked into beds and travel cots, in a first-floor bedroom. The older kids would be watching TV or playing games somewhere in the big house.

Inside he found Will and Becky's son, Nick, and Carly and Adam's boys playing a video game in the living room. "Hi, guys," he greeted them, and got grunts in return. They were all enthralled with their game and allowing themselves to be sidetracked would mean they could lose.

"Hi, Uncle Jack!" Luke's daughter Daisy called as she breezed through the room, followed by the clatter of feet on the stairs as her sister Celeste raced down to greet him.

"We've been waitin' ages 'n' ages for you!" Celeste told him. "Daddy says you've got a girlfriend."

Hoo, boy! The O'Malley telegraph was fully operational. He could picture it now—his parents and all his brothers and their wives lying in wait for him around the kitchen table.

He pushed open the kitchen door and saw that the situation was exactly as he'd suspected. Conversation ceased and eleven pairs of eyes swiveled in his direction. Even his nephew, Cody—who at seventeen was old enough to join the adults—was staring at him.

His mom looked at him expectantly. She leaned sideways a little as if to see whether anyone was following him.

"Hi, Mom. Sorry I'm late," he said as he crossed the room and bent to kiss her cheek. He should have brought flowers; they might have distracted her for a whole millisecond.

"Pop." He shook his father's hand, then made the rounds, exchanging kisses and handshakes.

They all sat down and looked at Jack.

After a full five seconds of silence, Will asked, "So where's Grace?"

"At her hotel." Jack glared at Adam. No secret was safe with an O'Malley.

"You should've invited her to dinner, dear," Sarah said, her voice filled with disappointment. "I made extra."

"Mom. Everybody," he said, looking at each relative in turn. "As you're no doubt aware, Grace is back in town. I've agreed to renovate the house she bought from her aunt Missy. End of conversation." He snatched up a bread roll and tore it in two. "I'm starving, Mom. What's for dinner?"

"That's it?" Sarah said as she placed bowls of fluffy mashed potatoes on the table, along with a huge salad. His father got up to carve a roast. Pop loved roast.

Sarah took her seat at the other end of the table.

"That's it?" she asked again. "You're not going to pick up where you two left off?"

"Mom! Please." He softened his tone, seeing the hurt in his mother's eyes. "She just got back here. I need to come to terms with that." He passed a plate loaded with slices of roast beef down the table.

"He's got a point," Matt, who was the county sheriff, said. "Grace Saunders broke my little brother's heart. I might go arrest her and throw her in jail until she makes a full confession of her sins."

"You just made a joke," Will observed. "A pathetic one, but it's not bad for you, big brother."

Everyone knew that Matt took life way too seriously, in free-spirited Will's opinion. "So where's she staying?" Will asked. "I'll ride shotgun."

"This is not the Wild West anymore," Will's wife, Becky, admonished. "But, if you'd like, I could beat her to a pulp with my interrogation tactics. Find out why she left a great guy like you. And why she *really* came back to Spruce Lake."

Jack smiled at Becky. She wasn't known for joking, either. "I appreciate your loyalty, but the truth is, she really *has* come back to renovate Missy Saunders's Victorian."

"And then she's going to flip it," Adam said with conviction as he piled mashed potatoes onto his plate.

"Grace is renovating it to save it from further ruin. She won't be selling it. The house has to stay in the family."

He turned his gaze back to Adam. "Have you remembered who Mike is yet?" he asked, then muttered, "Traitor," under his breath.

Carly grinned and said, "Jack, there's really no hurry to start building our house. For the moment, I'd prefer to stay closer to the hospital. And town. If Adam was on duty and I went into labor, at least he'd be close by."

"Not that he'd be any use," Luke, their oldest brother, said.

"Eat, everyone!" Sarah instructed. "Before it gets cold. We can ask Jack about his intentions toward Grace over dessert."

Jack groaned. And to think half an hour ago he'd been singing the praises of his close-knit family. He should've begged off coming here tonight, although, that would only have delayed the inevitable. When he and Grace were dating in high school, his parents and brothers had welcomed Grace into their lives. They'd been almost as devastated as he was when she'd accepted the scholarship to the college in Boston, and turned her back on Spruce Lake—and him.

While Grace seemed to have her life carefully mapped out, Jack had drifted from the peace corps to college, and then entered the seminary, believing that that was where he could best help others. But he'd felt there wasn't enough time for those genuinely in need. That was why he now helped train homeless and troubled youth in carpentry, to give them a skill, a job, a future. It was satisfying and both physically and emotionally exhausting, but Jack wouldn't have it any other way.

Thankfully, the focus was now off him as everyone ate and chatted about other topics. Next to him, Becky said, "I'd like to meet Grace sometime. I promise not to interrogate her."

Jack took a swig of beer and said, "I'd like to believe that, Becky. But I've seen you at social functions. Within five minutes of meeting someone, you know their name, occupation, hopes, dreams, likes and dislikes down to the most trivial facts of their existence."

"I do not!"

"Yeah, you do, sweetheart," Will said.

Everyone around the table murmured agreement. Becky harrumphed, then whispered to Jack, "Will told me a little about Grace. It sounds like she and I had a similar upbringing. I thought we could be friends. Maybe I could help ease her back into life in Spruce Lake."

Immediately Jack felt bad for misjudging Becky. She and Grace had both had fathers who were bums, they'd both moved around a lot growing up, they were supersmart and they'd won scholarships to college. And they were both divorced. Except Grace didn't have a child from her ill-fated marriage.

He said, "I'm sorry, Becky. You're right, of course. How about swinging by the old house tomorrow and I'll introduce you."

GRACE FLOPPED BACKWARD onto the bed in her hotel room. She hated hotels, their transient nature, accommodating you for a night or two and only too glad to see you on your way. That was why, when Jack had made the deal that meant she had to stay, she'd wanted to move into the house. To feel as if she had a home here until the renovation was finished and she went back to Boston.

She'd moved in with Edward when they got married, only buying a place of her own after the divorce.

They'd kept their money separate, which meant she'd saved a lot, but she'd also spent a lot on holidays of Edward's choosing.

"Fool!" she muttered. How gullible she'd been to sign a prenup that stated she was responsible for all her own expenses! She'd thought that meant her makeup and clothes, but once she was earning she was also responsible for her share of airfares, hotels and grocery bills. Edward would use his credit cards to purchase things, then bill her for her share. When she'd pointed out that he was claiming all the credit card reward points accrued for himself, he'd flown into such a rage she'd dropped it. She'd only realized years later that she'd been in an emotionally abusive relationship.

Grace blew out a breath, lifting her bangs off her forehead. She'd been so naive, marrying a man like that. "Never again!" she vowed, and headed to the shower.

Fifteen minutes later, she was in bed, after calling Marcie, the interior designer, and arranging to meet her at the house in the morning. Next, Grace reached into her purse and pulled out her wallet. She removed the photograph she kept there, tucked away where no one else could see it.

The photo had become worn around the edges over the years, so Grace had laminated it. She studied her newborn daughter. In the picture Grace was holding her close and gazing down at her, but Amelia was looking right at the camera, a tiny frown on her face.

Grace kissed the photo and returned it to her wallet, then closed her eyes and thought of what tomorrow would bring. More of Jack, she hoped. How different would her life have been if she'd stayed in Spruce Lake and married him? And kept their baby?

Chapter Five

When Grace arrived at the house at eight-thirty the following morning with Marcie Mason in tow, Jack had already replaced the broken windowpane, ordered the materials necessary to start the job and was just signing for a consignment of oak to fix the broken stair treads.

He gave one of his men a list of door and window locks to order, then went to meet the two women.

"Hi!" Grace greeted him as she alighted from her sleek red rental. "You fixed the window already!"

Jack ignored the instant effect Grace had on him, instead giving her a rundown of what had been achieved so far. "I've marked the steps that need replacing," he told them, "but be careful. If you don't mind, I'll leave you ladies to it, while I get on with making the new stairs."

Grace led the way to the second floor, chattering with Marcie like they were old friends. Satisfied, Jack set to work, doing a final measure of the treads.

Twenty minutes later, the two women were moving about the main floor, taking measurements and discussing color schemes.

Marcie disappeared into the kitchen, and Grace paused beside Jack. "She seems very competent," Grace said.

"More so than you," he said, nodding at her outfit. "I thought I told you to come dressed for work." He regretted the words the moment he said them. Being rude to Grace to cover his discomfort wasn't right.

"I was meeting an interior designer! I didn't want her getting the wrong impression of me."

"And what impression would that be?"

"That I let my contractor boss me around?"

"I'm so glad you made that a question," he said. "Once she leaves, you need to go buy a pair of boots like these." He indicated his heavy, steel-toed work boots.

Grace stared at them in horror. "You must be joking!"

"Nope. They're a health and safety requirement. And my requirement—which you agreed to, is that you pitch in and help. Remember?"

Grace screwed up her face. "Stuck between a rock and a hard place."

"Yup. And by the way, here's my estimate. In spite of your haste to get me going on this project, I think it only fair you should know what to expect."

Jack pulled several sheets of printed paper from his pocket and handed them to her. He watched as Grace scanned the pages, taking in all that needed to be done.

She looked up at last and said, "That's an awful lot of money. More than I expected..."

"This is an awful lot of house that hasn't been touched since it was built—apart from that eyesore of a seventies bathroom and kitchen renovation. This is the bare minimum it'll cost to renovate the place into something you can be proud of. If you want a cheap job, there are contractors who'll do it for you, but it won't be me."

"I don't remember you being this forthright at school."

"School was half our lifetimes ago. A lot has happened to both of us since then."

IT SURE HAS, Grace thought. *I had our baby, gave her away, then capped it off by marrying a complete Svengali— all to get away from my family, and what have I got to show for it?*

"Something wrong?" Jack asked.

Grace snapped back to the present. "No, everything's fine. Just don't order me around too much, okay? I need to find my own pace."

Jack frowned, but before he could ask about that revealing statement, Marcie reappeared.

"All done," she said. "I hope you accept my estimate, Grace. It'd be an honor to work on this place. It might even get a mention in the *Digest of American Architecture.*"

Jack groaned.

"What's wrong with that?" Grace demanded. "It's a very prestigious publication."

"Sorry, Jack," Marcie said. "I forgot about the fallout the last time you were featured in it."

Intrigued, Grace glanced from one to the other. "What? *What?*" she demanded.

"And that's my cue to leave," Marcie said, packing her notebook and tape measure into her briefcase. She waggled her fingers at them as she dashed through the front door.

Grace spun around to Jack. "Well? What was that about?"

"I got a bunch of, uh, fan mail when I was in that magazine a few years back."

"Which must have led to a lot of work for you. That's good!" she said, immensely pleased that her contractor was so talented he'd been featured in the magazine. Just wait until Edward and his horrible family saw her home in an upcoming issue! He'd tried to have their house highlighted several years ago, but the publication had rejected his bid. Probably because their mansion was more like a mausoleum than a home.

"All it led to was a lot of work dodging enthusiastic women. And some men," he said.

Grace started to giggle.

"Don't laugh! It was really distracting when so many people showed up at the work site asking for me. Luckily, Al fended most of them off."

"*Most* of them?" Grace nearly choked she was laughing so hard.

"Why is this so funny?" he demanded.

"Because you seem so unaware of your looks," she responded. "I guess I missed that issue. Tell me how they posed you for the photograph."

Jack widened his stance and crossed his arms.

Grace flushed. Jack's biceps, broad shoulders, black hair and vivid blue eyes made a pretty devastating combination. "I can see why you got so much fan mail," she said.

Jack scowled. "I wasn't posing like this," he said. "I'm crossing my arms because I'm refusing to discuss it."

"Wow! That must've been some photo," she said.

"I'm going to look it up online." Grace slung her bag over her shoulder and headed for the front door.

"Wait!"

She turned to see Jack blushing to the roots of his hair.

"It was that good, huh?" she teased.

"No, it was stupid. The photographer asked me to change. The photo they published was of me taking off my old shirt. It looked like a cheesy striptease."

Trying to lighten the situation she said, too flippantly, "No wonder you got so much attention. From both sexes."

"It wasn't funny at the time. And it still isn't. I take my work seriously."

Grace schooled her expression. Jack really felt hurt and she needed to respect that.

Changing the subject, she asked, "So, how are the rashes this morning?"

"Much better. I've quit the orange juice, and the cream is giving me a lot of relief." He rolled up his sleeve to show her. "Looks fifty percent better already."

Grace brushed his inner elbow with her fingertip. She noticed him flinching. Surely Jack wasn't that unused to a woman's touch?

A sudden wolf whistle surprised her and she jumped back from him, searching for the culprit.

"Tyrone!" Jack shouted.

A lanky black youth sauntered over, grinning from ear to ear. "Yes, boss?" he said.

"Don't ever do that to a client again. In fact, to any woman. It's disrespectful. Now apologize to Dr. Saunders."

The kid raised one finger to his head in a salute. "Sorry, ma'am."

Jack turned to Grace. "This is Tyrone. He's one of my apprentices, and since he's only been here a couple of weeks, he hasn't been fully house-trained yet." He cuffed the kid gently on the shoulder and said, "Get back to work."

"Sure, boss, and sorry again, ma'am." Tyrone went back to planing some timber.

"Actually, I wasn't all that offended. Especially since he's just a harmless kid," Grace said.

"Ten weeks ago that kid was serving time in juvie for pulling a knife on a shopkeeper."

Grace paled. "Oh."

Then she glanced around at the rest of the young men working on her house. They all seemed a little rough around the edges.

"I can see your mind working," Jack said. "Let me assure you that underneath the tough exteriors, they're just kids who need a chance."

"And you know this because…"

"So far I've trained about forty kids who were either homeless or headed for jail. All of them now have jobs in the building trade all over the States. Some have even started their own businesses."

"I had no idea you did this."

Jack shrugged. "Why would you?"

"I, uh…" Grace's life suddenly looked awfully shallow from where she was standing. What had she ever done to give back to the community? "Am I taking you away from helping them? By hiring you to work on my home?"

"Nope. This is the perfect project for them. Come and meet the rest of the guys. They don't bite."

Grace stayed where she was. "I feel a little foolish dressed like this when I'm supposed to be part of the crew. Should I change into work clothes first?"

"No, it's better they meet you in all your prissiness, and then when you get changed they'll realize you're human, too."

Grace rolled her eyes at his mild chastisement. "Okay, then. Lead the way," she said.

They went inside and up the stairs where one of the boys was working on her banister railings.

"Dr. Saunders, meet Zac. He's been with me for over a year and is shaping up to be a fine carpenter."

"Please, call me Grace," she said, offering her hand to Zac, a short, bespectacled kid whom Grace couldn't imagine ever being in trouble with the law. He seemed too...*normal.* Or was she just seeing the glasses and equating them with being studious?

He shook her hand. "Nice to meet you, ma'am. Jack said you're going to pitch in around the job site."

He looked a little too long at Grace's totally inappropriate attire and she felt it necessary to joke, "I guess heels are a no-no?"

Zac shrugged. "Whatever the boss says."

Something crashed downstairs. She and Jack raced to the first floor to find dust billowing out of the kitchen. As it cleared, Grace saw that half the cabinets had been torn from the wall.

A huge man stood in the midst of the debris.

"This is Ace. He specializes in demolition," Jack said with a wry smile.

"Grace," she said, shaking hands with the tall, well-built young man sporting tattoos on his arms and shoulders.

"This your house, ma'am?" he asked.

"Yes," she said, taking in the wreckage. The old seventies cabinets were hideous, but at least they'd hidden the wall. Now that it was exposed, she could see it was covered in years of built-up grime.

"Ace has only been with me a couple of weeks, so I'm not letting him near the power tools yet."

Ace grinned, revealing a missing front tooth. Grace feared he'd be missing some digits if he went anywhere near a power tool.

"My other two apprentices have a couple of days off. They're my most experienced men, and one of them will be taking Ace under his wing."

"I thought *you* were going to be working on my house," Grace said.

"I will. But I'm a contractor, which means I have a lot more to do than hammering nails and cutting lumber. I teach the guys and do the finer work myself. Al is the foreman and he keeps an eye on them. Don't worry, your house is in good hands—the entire crew just finished building a new house. Renovating a Victorian is a real challenge and they're all up for it."

They walked outside, escaping the sound of more crashing as Ace got back to cabinet demolition.

A truck with a Dumpster on its flatbed was looking for a parking space farther down the street.

"It would help if you moved your car," Jack pointed out. "Go change and I'll see you back here in an hour. No later, okay?"

"*Who* exactly is the boss here?" she demanded.

"I am," Jack said unequivocally. "And what I say goes. You're just the owner. Now get going."

If he hadn't said it with a smile, Grace might have been offended. Instead, she bustled to her car and waved at the Dumpster delivery guy to indicate he could have her spot.

JACK SHOOK HIS HEAD as Grace drove away. Already he regretted his request that she roll up her sleeves and pitch in. Working in such close proximity with Grace wasn't one of his best ideas. Yet from the moment he'd laid eyes on her again, he'd wanted her back in his life. But he needed to forgive her first.

Forgiveness didn't come easily to Jack, in spite of his time in the seminary. It might have had something to do with the two weeks he spent on life support after being assaulted and knifed by gang members. The memory of Jayden Tyler, the kid he'd tried so hard to save from the gang, walking away from him as he lay bleeding in that L.A. alley, had never stopped haunting him. The fact that someone he'd put so much faith in could be so callous still burned his guts.

Pushing the memories away, Jack went inside and ascended to the attic to check the roof for leaks.

Chapter Six

They were ugly. Unbelievably ugly. Grace groaned at the steel-toed boots Jack had insisted she purchase to wear on the job site. She had half a mind to tell him to forget it. Footwear this hideous was almost a deal breaker; she was half-tempted to tell him she was going to Europe instead.

But Grace wasn't a quitter—well, apart from quitting her pediatric practice to trek halfway across the country on a whim. And she hadn't really quit, she was taking an extended leave. She'd arranged with other pediatricians at the practice to cover her caseload.

A couple of attractive college-age girls sauntered past the store window and it gave Grace an idea. So Mr. Jack O'Malley thought he could ignore his attraction to her, did he?

JACK FELT THE SUCKER punch the moment Grace stepped out of her car and strolled along the sidewalk and through the front gate. He'd been watching for her car as he worked on the front porch, showing Tyrone how to fix the railings. Of course, he could've been working anywhere else on the property, but the front porch was the perfect place to keep an eye on Grace's arrival.

And now he was glad he had because he needed to stop her before she took another step.

Instead of the coveralls he'd expected, Grace wore a tight-fitting, scoop-neck T-shirt that left nothing to the imagination, denim shorts and puffy white socks. The only thing she'd complied with were the requisite boots. The scant clothing teamed with the boots was an incredibly sexy combination.

Jack tried to swallow the baseball-size lump in his throat and said, "Hold it right there!"

Unfortunately, Tyrone chose that moment to look up and managed half a wolf whistle before Jack spun around and silenced him with a glare.

"Sorry, ma'am. Boss," he said, not sounding the least bit sorry and not taking his eyes off Grace.

Jack positioned himself to block Tyrone's view and growled at her, "What the *hell* do you think you're wearing? Take those off at once!"

"If you insist," she said with a cheeky smile, and reached for the hem of her T-shirt.

Jack grabbed her hand, preventing her from lifting her arms.

"Are you crazy?" he demanded.

Jack took her by the elbow and steered her out the gate and down the sidewalk to Betsy. He wrenched open the door. "Get in," he growled.

Grace obeyed without protest. He slammed the door shut with more force than needed, then rounded the old truck and got into the driver's seat. He rested his left arm on the wheel and turned to her. "What do you think you're doing?"

He swore she batted her eyelids as she asked, "Doing?"

"Yeah, *doing.* Coming to a job site dressed like a *Playboy* centerfold."

Grace's eyebrows rose at that. "You read *Playboy?* A good Catholic-raised boy like you?"

"Grace!"

"Anyway, centerfolds are naked. But thanks for the compliment. I think."

He cursed under his breath, started Betsy up, put her in gear and pulled out onto the street.

"Where are we going?"

"To buy you some coveralls. You can't work on the house dressed like that."

"But it's a hot day! I thought shorts would be perfect. I don't want to wear sweaty old coveralls."

The image of Grace getting sweaty in coveralls was almost as sexy as the shorts. Except then he wouldn't be able to see her legs. Her beautiful long legs that he suddenly wanted wrapped around him.

Day one of the job and he already had a conflict with a client. A *serious* conflict.

He pulled off the road and drove down to the river where they'd have some privacy.

He cut the engine and turned to her again. "Let me spell this out for you in case you missed it this morning. That job site is swarming with young men, some still in their teens. Young men have active hormones. It's not a good idea to overstimulate them by wearing suggestive clothing. It's unfair."

Grace undid her seat belt and leaned toward him. Suddenly Betsy's wide bench seat didn't seem so wide.

"The only person who was getting *overstimulated* was you, Jack."

Jack ground his teeth together so tightly he could feel a headache coming on. "Tyrone was there, too."

"Tyrone's just a boy. You're a man."

"You need to cover up. That's nonnegotiable."

She smiled and he felt that sucker punch deep in his gut.

Some perverse curiosity made him ask, "Why did you dress like this? Seriously."

Grace had always been a conservative dresser in high school. He'd barely seen her legs except at swim meets. And he'd liked what he'd seen. Now he liked it even more. She'd worn the clothes to make him react. Did that mean…?

"You're staring," she purred, placing her hand on his thigh.

Jack swallowed and forced his eyes to meet hers. Bad move. Her lashes were lowered, her mouth pouted. And then she licked her lips.

Suddenly he was reaching for her, his hands beneath her butt, lifting her to straddle his lap. Grace wrapped her arms around his neck, leaving his mouth nowhere to go but against her throat. He kissed the soft skin there and she moaned.

She kissed his forehead, the bridge of his nose. He raised his mouth to meet hers and kissed her with all the love he'd held in his heart. The realization that he still loved her shook Jack to the core. This was Grace, the woman he'd *never* stopped loving, if he was honest about it. He took what he wanted and demanded more.

And Grace, bless her, met him halfway and gave and gave and gave.

Jack pulled her hard against him. Grace complied by wriggling even farther into his lap as they kissed like desperate teenagers—and adult lovers. It was the most erotic moment of Jack's life and he never wanted it to end. So much for keeping his distance, so much for his principles.

Grace tore her mouth from his and said, her voice raspy with desire, "Your place or mine?"

It took time for the sexual fog to clear and for Jack to process her words. When he did, it was as if a wet blanket had been thrown over him. Reluctantly, he lifted Grace off his lap and placed her on the seat as he fought to calm his breathing.

She frowned in confusion and he wanted to stroke that indentation between her pretty brows away.

"I don't…I don't have relationships with clients," he managed to say.

Smiling with relief Grace asked, "Who said anything about a relationship? This is sex, Jack. No strings attached."

They were exactly the words he didn't want to hear. Not from Grace—*especially* not from Grace. He slid behind the wheel and gripped it as though afraid that if he didn't, he'd be pulling Grace into his arms again and damn his principles.

"I don't do no-strings-attached sex, sweetheart."

Her eyes widened at the endearment and he wished he could take it back. He couldn't get in any deeper with Grace, couldn't let her know he still loved her. Couldn't let his heart be broken a second time.

"Oh, come on, Jack! We're adults now, not fumbling virgins making out at Inspiration Point. We're both single, so what's the harm?"

More harm than you could ever imagine, he thought as she reached out and touched the exposed skin above his collar. He longed to hold her hand over his heart but instead he caught it and placed it on the seat between them.

"We'd better go. I have work to do," he said as he started Betsy.

"And I don't?"

He glanced over at her. "It's pretty obvious you think this is some kind of game. Since you aren't prepared to come to work dressed appropriately, it's best if you stay away from the job site altogether."

"You must be joking! That's *my* house. You can't keep me away!"

"Maybe not. But if you ever come to the site dressed like that again, you can find yourself another contractor."

HIS WORDS FELT LIKE a slap in the face. A couple of minutes ago, Jack was kissing her as though she was the last woman on earth and now he was threatening to quit?

Tears burned the backs of her eyes.

"What did I do wrong?" she asked shakily.

He cut the ignition. "What part of 'you can't dress like that for work' did you not understand?"

"I don't mean that!" she snapped, the tears gone. "Why don't you want to make love to me?"

Jack stared out the windshield for a frustratingly long time. So long that Grace became aware of the sounds of the river rushing by, birds twittering in the willows, vehicles lumbering along the road above them, kids playing baseball. Everything seemed amplified and she wanted to close Betsy's window, shut it all out so there was only her and Jack. But Betsy was so ancient she didn't have air-conditioning, and the day was getting hotter.

"I already told you. I don't sleep with clients," he said, starting Betsy up again. Her wheels spun on the gravel as he turned and drove to the main road. At the intersection he stopped and said, "Do I go left to the hardware store for some coveralls for you, or right and back to town?"

"Where am I more likely to find another contractor?"

Without missing a beat, he said, "Probably at the hardware store. Guys looking for work leave their cards there all the time." Not waiting for her answer, he went left.

She crossed her arms and slouched in the seat. "When you're no longer my contractor, we can finish what we started back there."

"Whether I'm you're contractor or not, I don't do casual sex, Grace. Never have. Never will."

She sat up and glared at him. "You're making me sound like some kind of skank!"

He shrugged, which only infuriated her further. They parked outside the hardware store. "I'll drop you off here to check out some leads. Since you no longer need my services, I have to get back to the house and pull the guys off the job." He opened his glove box, found a business card and handed it to her. "This is the local cab company. You can take a taxi back to the house to get your car."

"You can't leave me here like this!"

"You want another contractor. I don't have time to wait around while you find one."

Tears of confusion burned the backs of Grace's eyes. What the hell had she done? She'd called his bluff and it had come back to bite her on the butt. Not wanting him to see her cry or realize how much he'd hurt her, Grace snatched the card from his fingers. Then she opened Betsy's door, climbed out and marched into the store.

JACK STARED AT HER retreating back, noticing her cute butt as she sashayed across the parking lot.

Her words had bitten deep, but he'd been determined not to show her he cared. He'd wanted to work on the old house, but he couldn't do it playing cat-and-mouse with Grace. If she wanted to fire him, it was her right.

He cursed and hit the steering wheel. What the hell had he just done?

Chapter Seven

Jack pulled out his cell phone and punched in Al's number.

"What's up, boss?" his foreman asked. "Having trouble taming that little filly?"

"She fired us."

"*What the hell?* What did you do to her?" Al demanded.

"It's not going to work, that's all. So start packing up and get the men ready to move on to Adam's house."

"I thought your brother didn't want his house built yet."

"He was being polite," Jack growled.

"But I just got a huge load of lumber delivered."

"We'll bill her for it. Not our problem anymore. Pack up the site. I'll be back in twenty minutes."

"But—"

Jack cut the connection. He was in no mood to argue with Al. No mood for anything except maybe a long ride at the ranch. He called Luke.

"Hey, Jack, what's up?" his oldest brother answered.

"Where are you?" Jack asked without preamble.

"Mending fences up in paddock seven. Why?"

"I'll meet you there. That okay?"

"Sure, but aren't you working today?"

"Not anymore," Jack said, and disconnected.

He called Al back and said, "Once you've cleaned up the job site, give the guys the rest of the day off. I'll talk to you later this evening. And tell the guys I'll see them tomorrow."

He put away his cell and watched the doors of the hardware store, willing Grace to come out. That was a lousy thing to do, giving her the cab company's card. Maybe he should go in and find her. He shouldn't have let her go in the store dressed like that. The place was full of men. And men liked to stare at pretty girls, especially half-dressed ones.

GRACE HAD GONE straight to the restroom inside the store. She slammed the door of a stall, sat on the toilet and let the tears flow. What was Jack's problem? He'd fired her? Just because she wanted sex?

Lord, how she wanted him! She'd been more turned on in those couple of minutes with Jack than she'd ever been during her entire lousy excuse of a marriage.

Maybe she didn't turn him on in the same way? That thought produced a fresh flood of tears.

"Hello? Are you okay?"

Grace heard a woman's voice outside the stall. She grabbed a handful of toilet paper and blew her nose.

"I'm fine," she muttered.

"You don't sound fine, honey," the woman said. "Come on out and let's talk."

"I...don't want...to talk. I just want to...to cry."

"You can do both. Come on. I'm a good listener," the woman said. "It's a man, isn't it?"

"How…did you know?" Grace asked, and blew her nose again.

"Usually is."

Grace stood and flushed away the paper. She opened the door and went to the sinks to wash her hands and splash water on her face. The woman offered her a wad of paper towels.

"Name's Sally," the woman said.

"Thanks," she said, taking the towels and blotting away her tears. "I'm Grace."

"Pretty little thing like you shouldn't be crying over a man."

At five-eight, Grace had never been described as little, but since Sally towered over her by a good few inches, she guessed she could let that slip. Sally looked to be in her late thirties. She was broad-shouldered, fair-haired and freckled, and had the look of a woman who worked hard. Her nails were short, her hands weathered.

Grace forced a smile. "I don't know why I gave in to that pity party. I never cry!"

Sally patted her shoulder. "You cried because you care. So who is he? I'll go track him down and break an arm or something."

Grace's smile relaxed. "No need to do that. Although I'm tempted to smack him in the head with a frying pan."

"Hmm," Sally said, "So he hasn't so much broken your heart as bruised your ego?"

Grace thought about that. Sally was right. "How did you get so wise?" she asked. She bent to splash water on her face again, then looked into the mirror. She was a mess.

Sally held out more paper towels. "Feel like talking about it over a coffee?" she asked.

"How about I buy you lunch instead?" Grace offered. "I think my situation will take longer to explain than that. And I'm starving."

"Done! What are you driving so I can follow you?"

"I don't have a car here. He and I sort of...parted ways in the parking lot."

"This is getting more interesting by the minute," Sally said. "And it sounds like he really does need a frying pan to the head. Come on, we'll take my truck. I know a great place to eat."

"So you've had a fight with Grace already?" Luke said as Jack dismounted.

"How'd you know?"

"Al called, said she'd fired you and that you'd be starting on Adam's house in the morning. I thought Adam didn't want his house built yet?"

"Tough," Jack said, picking up a pair of pliers to help mend the fence.

"Why'd she fire you?" Luke asked. One thing about Jack's brothers, they could be downright blunt.

Jack decided to be equally blunt. "Because I wouldn't sleep with her."

Luke's head snapped up and for the first time he stopped working. "Whoa! When did this happen—or, rather, not happen?"

Jack refused to answer and instead concentrated on the fence.

"Why don't you want to sleep with her? She's turned into quite something."

"How would you know?" As far as Jack was aware, Luke and Grace's paths hadn't crossed since she'd returned.

Luke shrugged. "Al."

Jack cursed as he worked the wire.

"Did you two ever do the deed in high school?"

"That is *so* none of your business, I'm not going to answer it."

"Don't need to, you just did."

Jack ran his hand through his hair, wishing he'd worn a hat. The sun was beating down as if it was already mid-August. "I told her I don't sleep with clients."

Luke grinned. "So she fired you and now you *can* sleep with her. Smart girl."

"You have such a simplistic view of life. I have no idea how we're even related."

"Because our parents had sex."

"Very funny."

"I'm known across three counties for my sense of humor," Luke said.

"No, you're not. You never crack a joke."

"Megan's been teaching me."

Jack had to concede that since he'd married Megan, Luke had lightened up. A lot. He'd been married to one of the worst women on earth and now he was married to one of the best. Luke and Megan had met during a holiday romance eighteen years earlier, and it had taken them a long time to find each other again.

"So, now that you're no longer her contractor, why aren't you two steaming up the bedroom?"

"You're so crude."

"And curious. I've got Will on speed dial. He wants to hear what's up, too."

"How did Will get involved in this?"

"He stopped by the old house just after you took off. Tyrone told him you and Grace left in a big hurry. Naturally, with Will's overactive imagination, he's dreaming up all sorts of scenarios. Most of them probably wrong."

"This conversation doesn't go beyond this paddock?" Jack insisted.

"O-kay," Luke conceded. "But I want all the details."

"There are no 'details' and you wouldn't get them if there were," Jack said as they started to pack up their tools, then mounted up and rode along the fence line looking for breaks.

"I don't do casual sex." Jack said it brusquely, repeating what he'd said to Grace—and referring to Luke's wild ways when he was in college.

"Maybe you're right. We aren't related, after all," Luke said with a wink.

Jack ground his teeth. Talking to Luke hadn't been such a great idea, after all. He should've seen Matt instead. Matt would take the matter seriously. Matt would probably have some good advice. He dug into his horse's flanks and took off across the paddock, needing to feel the wind against his face. Hoping it would help clear his head. What was wrong with him? He and Grace were adults, so why not make the most of it while Grace was in town and then they could part with no regrets.

Because you love her, his inner voice echoed as he slowed his horse and then began to pick their way through the boulders littering the hillside. *You've only ever loved her.*

He halted his mount and took in the scenery unfolding below him. They were so high up here, Jack could see all the way to the next county. The ranch house at Two Elk, where he'd grown up with his four brothers, lay in the valley to the left of him. Leading away from the ranch was the road to town, which forked in the other direction to the valley where Will and Matt lived with their families and where Adam would settle with his family when Jack built him a home there.

Meanwhile, Jack lived in an old miner's shack he'd converted at the far end of the same valley. It had been a burned-out shell that had proven to be a good project for his apprentices, a lesson in preserving and restoring old buildings. Most of them had laughed when he'd driven them out there to start the job, but by the end of it, they'd all taken pride in what they'd done. In the process, they'd learned the history of the area and the hardships the early settlers had endured to scratch a living from the land. The settlers' perseverance against the worst that the landscape and life could throw at them had been a salient lesson for many of the kids....

He heard Luke's horse approach, his hoofs scraping the boulders.

"Sorry I was so flippant before, buddy," his brother said. "I keep forgetting how different you and I are."

"'S'okay."

"You're still in love with her, aren't you?"

"Yup."

"And you're scared of getting hurt when she leaves town again?"

"Yup."

"But how will you feel if she leaves town in a couple of months and you never told her how you really feel?"

Chapter Eight

"The way I'm reading this," Sally said, putting down the rib she'd been chewing on, "is not so much that Jack doesn't want to make love to you, but that he wants it to be more than a quick roll in the hay." She picked up another rib. "He sounds like a keeper to me."

"Except that I don't want a keeper," Grace said. "I don't want to get seriously involved with anyone. No one will dictate my life ever again."

Sally's low whistle made several heads in Rusty's turn their way. She ignored them, saying, "I hear Jack O'Malley's good people, though."

With a sigh, Grace tossed the corn chip she'd been playing with onto her plate of nachos and leaned back in the booth. "He is. Really good. Too good for me, I think."

"Don't go selling yourself short. This relationship is worth salvaging."

"There is no relationship!" Grace said more forcefully than she meant to. "Jack and I dated back in high school. And now, we're…ancient history."

Sally sat forward, her lunch forgotten. "Were you doing more than just *dating* in high school?"

Grace chuckled at Sally's enthusiasm. She'd barely

known this woman for thirty minutes and had already confessed pretty much everything about her lousy marriage and her initial reasons for returning to Spruce Lake. And now Sally wanted the details of her history with Jack.

The only women she'd associated with in Boston had been colleagues. She'd kept her private life private, but there was something about Sally, something totally guileless, that had Grace wanting to confess all, as if they were long-time friends rather than two people who'd met in the restroom of a local hardware store half an hour earlier.

"No, we weren't intimate—until the night before he left to join the peace corps somewhere in Guatemala," Grace admitted.

"I'd heard he was a priest or something?"

"You seem to know a bit about him."

Sally shrugged. "Just gossip. I've only been living here a couple of months, but his name has come up in conversation. Folks are impressed by what he does to get wayward teens back on track, how principled he is."

"Pity his principles extend to me." She sighed. "I only came here for the house. I never expected that Jack still lived here, nor that my lawyer had asked him to do an estimate. Hell, I didn't even know he was a contractor. But when I saw Jack, all grown up and virile as hell, my priorities took a right turn."

Sally grinned. "Just because he turned you down doesn't mean he isn't into sex. You'll have to go seduce him some other way."

"Which isn't going to happen now because we're not even on speaking terms."

"Hey! Some of the best sex my husband and I have is makeup sex."

They shared a laugh at that, and Grace said, "I'm sorry, I've been wailing about all my problems and never bothered to find out a thing about you, Sally. Tell me about your husband."

"Dex and I were high school sweethearts. I ended up pregnant, so we got married and here I am."

Grace raised her eyebrows. "I think your story is a little more detailed than that. Do you have more children? Have you always lived in Colorado?"

Sally wiped her mouth with her napkin and pushed her plate away. "Dex and I grew up in a small town in Kansas. After we got married we lived with my parents until we both finished high school. Dex did odd jobs around town. We couldn't afford college, but he started working for a roofing contractor, learned the business and started his own. A few years later, we sold it and moved to Denver, bought a home, had a couple more kids. Our youngest has bad asthma and Denver was too polluted, so we hunted around for somewhere with clean air, good schools and a low crime rate. Spruce Lake area seemed perfect, so we rented out our place in Denver and signed a lease on a house in Harper's Corner. Once we know exactly where we want to put down roots, we'll sell the Denver house and buy here." She grimaced. "Or at least that's the plan. There was plenty of work until recently, but now it's not so great. We might have to move back to Denver or somewhere even farther afield for work."

"And you don't want that?"

"Nope, we both love it here. And we worry about how

our son will cope where the air isn't mountain-fresh and clear. You know much about asthma, Grace?"

Grace hadn't yet mentioned her area of specialty, just told Sally she was a doctor and had been married to a surgeon. "Actually, I'm a pediatrician."

Sally's eyes widened with interest. "Well, I'll be… If you have any insights on the latest research, I'd love to hear them. And the town could do with your skills."

Grace didn't want to disappoint Sally by telling her she was leaving town as soon as she could hand the renovation over to another contractor, so she let it ride.

"Speak of the devil," Sally muttered. "If that isn't one of the prettiest sights in Spruce Lake. Yessiree. Not one gorgeous man, but two."

Grace spun around in the booth to see what Sally was talking about.

Jack—and Matt, the county sheriff—had just entered Rusty's. Her face burning, she spun back to face Sally before Jack noticed her.

Fortunately, he didn't. Unfortunately, Sally was grinning from ear to ear and motioning them over.

"Sally!" she hissed. "I don't want to see him."

But Sally ignored her. "Sheriff Matt, how lovely to see you again," she said, offering her hand for him to shake. "How's that beautiful wife of yours?"

Sally knew Matt O'Malley enough to ask after his wife? Why hadn't she mentioned this earlier? Grace sure wouldn't have spilled her guts about Jack had she known.

"She's well, thanks, Sally. And Dex?"

"Great. He's working in Silver Springs this week, so I'm doing the books and visiting the hardware store to pick up supplies." She indicated Grace, who was study-ing the remains of her lunch. "I think you might have already met my friend Grace Saunders."

Grace glanced up at Matt, avoiding Jack's eyes. She was all too aware of him standing beside his brother, taking up way too much space in the tiny restaurant. Robbing her of air. Preventing her escape.

"Well, well," Matt said. "Jack and I were just talking about you, Grace. Mind if we join you?" he asked and, without waiting for an answer, sat down beside Sally.

Sally, the traitor, slid over to accommodate him. Grace had no intention of making room for Jack and refused to move.

"We're taking a late lunch," Matt explained. "Nice to have some company. Can we order you ladies another drink?" He gestured to a young waiter who practically raced to their table. Anything to keep the county sher-iff happy, it seemed.

"I won't say no to another root beer," Sally said. "Grace and I have been talking so much, I'm parched."

Great! Why don't you just tell them everything we've been talking about, Grace nearly blurted.

"Four root beers," Matt said to the waiter. "Make mine a diet and I'll have a Cobb salad with grilled chicken. What'll you have, Jack? And for heaven's sake, sit down."

Since he was given no other option, Jack complied, sitting beside Grace, who scooted over so far she was practically glued to the wall on the other side. "Burger and fries," he muttered.

"I'm not sure if you've met my brother, Sally," Matt said. "Jack's a contractor. Jack, this is Sally Carter. Her husband Dex is a roofing contractor. Maybe you could send some work his way?"

Jack nodded at Sally. "Nice to meet you, I've heard good things about Dex's work. If you have his card, I'll get an estimate from him for my next job."

"Jack's supposed to be working on Grace's house, but she fired him this morning," Matt said to Sally as if the other two weren't there.

"I did not fire him!" Grace spoke up at last. "He fired me!"

Matt's eyes narrowed. "Is this true, Jack? One day on the job and already you're fighting with the client?" He grinned then and Grace suspected Matt was all bluster, not taking the matter nearly as seriously as he was pretending.

"Stay out of it, Matt," Jack warned.

Grace grabbed her purse, ready to get out of there. One problem—Jack was blocking the way.

"Stay right where you are, Grace," Matt said. "Neither of you is leaving until you've both said sorry to each other and shaken hands on it."

"The hell I will!" Grace said, crossing her arms. "I have nothing to apologize for. It's your Neanderthal brother who's causing all the trouble."

Matt nodded sagely and looked at Jack. "She's probably right. You've had so little experience with women, you have no idea how to treat them."

The statement surprised Grace. Jack hadn't had a lot of girlfriends?

"And you just stepped *way* over the line," Jack said, rising.

Matt reached across the table and pushed him back

down. "Food's here," he said, then stole one of Jack's fries and had his wrist slapped by his brother. With a grin, Matt popped the French fry in his mouth, his expression blissful.

The fries smelled so good, Grace was tempted to steal one herself.

Matt looked in disgust at his salad, then dug his fork in. Grace was thankful the crisp vegetables would have him chewing for a while, unable to demand one or the other of them to apologize. Not so with Sally, however. She'd long since finished her ribs, declared them delicious and was ready to play devil's advocate. "So who's going to say they're sorry first and when are you starting work on Grace's house again, Jack?"

Jack glanced at Grace. "My rules still stand. Unless you're prepared to agree to them, we don't have a business contract."

"Rules?" Matt and Sally asked at once, both leaning forward.

"Grace knows them and that's all that matters," Jack snapped.

"Okay, I agree to the rules," Grace conceded. "But you have to agree to use Sally's husband for the roofing."

"And if his estimate comes in too high?" Jack asked.

"It won't," Sally told him. "I'm sure Dex would love to work on such a beautiful building. Apart from that, we have three kids to feed, so we could do with the work. Speaking of which, I need to collect them from school." She began to stand and Matt got up to let her by. Shaking Jack's hand, she said, "Great to meet you at last, Jack. And a pleasure meeting you, Grace." She removed a couple of business cards from her wallet, handing one to Jack and the other to Grace. "Give me a call sometime. I live in a houseful of men, so it's nice to have some girl talk."

"Thanks for coming to my rescue," Grace said, looking pointedly at Jack. "I don't know how I would have got back into town without your help, Sally. And I look forward to meeting the rest of your family."

Matt slid back into the booth as she left and said, "I didn't realize Sally was so lonely. I'll have Beth give her a call and invite them over for dinner one night."

"I don't like the way you keep puffing every time you move, big brother," Jack said, observing Matt's shortness of breath. "You need more exercise. Starting tomorrow morning, you and I are hiking up the peak. Meet me at the base at six."

"You've gotta be kidding! You want to kill me? I wouldn't make it to the halfway station."

"Then that'll be our goal the first day. You want to be able to eat fries again sometime this century, don't you?"

Matt looked so forlorn, Grace couldn't help laughing. "I do seem to remember you as the action-man of the family, Matt."

"He's gone from chasing the bad guys to too much administration."

"If I had the time, I'd go to the gym," Matt said, defending himself.

"Forget the gym. What you need is good, clean mountain air. I might bring a couple of the guys along, too. I think Tyrone would enjoy the exercise. And the views."

Matt nodded. "Growing up, the only exercise he got

was running away from the cops and gangs. And until you took him on, the only view he was likely to get was from a jail cell in Dade County."

"He's a good kid. He was heartbroken when you decided you no longer needed our services," he said, looking at Grace.

"Enough already!" she said, holding up her hands. "I've agreed to your stupid rules. Now lay off."

Jack shrugged and took the last bite of his burger.

"So are you two going to start dating again?" Matt asked, obviously trying to feign innocence.

Jack almost choked on his burger at Matt's question, so Grace said, "No, we aren't. Now if you'll excuse me, I have overalls to buy." She stood up, forcing Jack to move over so she could get out of the booth.

"You want a ride back to the house?" he asked.

"It's two blocks. I'm sure I can make it all by my little bitty self, thank you," she snapped, and dropped a couple of twenties on the table to cover her and Sally's bill.

"I'd like to meet Beth, Matt. Here's my card. She can call me anytime. Or just ask her to drop by the house. She might find me covered in sawdust," she said, glaring at Jack, "but it would be a pleasure to meet the woman who snagged a catch like you."

Matt glowed under her compliment and Jack's jaw dropped. "What about me?" he finally managed.

"You're not married," she said. "And the way you treat women, I doubt you ever will be."

With that, she turned on her steel-toed boot and strolled out of the restaurant, careful to put a little more sway into her hips than necessary.

MATT CHUCKLED AS he watched her leave.

"I have a feeling, little brother, that your rule about not sleeping with a client is going to be broken very soon."

Chapter Nine

Damn Matt. Damn Sally, and especially, damn Grace!
Jack thought as he drove back to the house. Fortunately,
Grace's car was no longer parked out front, so he didn't
have to see her. What he hadn't expected to see was the
place swarming with his workers.

"What's going on?" he asked Al. "Didn't I tell you
to clear this site?"

"You did. But then the guys wanted to stay. You
know how much they want to work on a house like this.
I couldn't leave them unsupervised. Plus, I knew one of
your brothers would talk some sense into you. That's
why I called Luke."

Jack grunted and stormed inside. Ace had already
demolished the kitchen, leaving a bare shell. Jack was
impressed by the speed with which he worked. Ace and
Tyrone were sweeping up the last of the dust.

"Good job, Ace," he said, going over to the young
man and clapping him on the shoulder. Jack took the
broom from him and said, "Take the rest of the afternoon off. You and the guys go to Rusty's and have a
meal on me. I'll see you all at seven tomorrow and we
can start fresh."

"So you and Ms. Grace are friends again?" Ace said.

News traveled fast around Spruce Lake. Al wouldn't have said anything to the guys, so he wondered how they knew. His question was answered as his brother Will meandered down the stairs and said, "Heard you were having woman trouble, so I stopped by to help."

Jack glared at him. "You can help by getting off this job site. And don't play with any of the power tools on your way out!" he said to Will's retreating back. Will had a reputation for being clumsy with tools, but strap on a pair of skis and the guy couldn't make a wrong move.

"Catch you Friday, buddy," Will said as he sauntered out the front door. "Oh, and Mom said to bring Grace."

Will was referring to the regular Friday-night gathering at Two Elk. He was certainly *not* taking Grace. With all his brothers, their spouses and his mom campaigning for him and Grace to pick up where they'd left off fourteen years ago, Jack was sure he didn't stand a chance. He wanted to win Grace back by fair means, not through his family's interference.

"I'M DYIN' HERE," Matt puffed as they hiked up Mount Sourdough, one of the four ski mountains surrounding Spruce Lake.

"No, you're just out of shape," Jack told him, not even breathing heavily. "After this, I'm going to work on Grace's house, while you'll be going to a breakfast meeting. If you want to have a doughnut that Beth won't hear about, then you'll shut up and walk."

"When…did you…get so…bossy?" Matt panted.

"Since my brothers decided to stick their noses into my love life."

"So you admit...you're still in love with Grace?"

"Just keep walking."

"I don't understand why you're so reluctant to make the most of the time she's here. What's the problem?"

Jack stopped and looked at him. "Because I don't work that way. I never have and never will!" Deciding they'd gone high enough for one day, he turned to start walking downhill, then halted and pivoted back to Matt.

"My relationship with Grace is none of your business, Matt, and that's how I want it to stay."

"Hey! You're the one who said you needed to talk yesterday and we ended up at Rusty's."

"Where you proceeded to humiliate me by demanding I apologize to Grace."

Matt shook his head. "Oh, little brother, you have a long way to go if you haven't learned the two most important words for trying to placate a woman."

"And what are they?"

"Yes, dear."

"Very funny," Jack said, increasing the pace and forcing Matt to keep up.

"You should bring Grace up here for a picnic," Matt said. "Bet all these wildflowers spread out like a carpet would have her eating out of your hand."

"I don't want her eating out of my hand."

"What do you want from her, then? If it isn't sex, then what?"

Jack stopped so suddenly, Matt almost barreled into him. "I want what you and Beth have, Mom and Pop, Luke and Megan, Adam and Carly. Even Will and Becky, although what she ever saw in him is beyond me."

"Such harsh criticism from you? Our most compassionate brother?"

Jack ignored the remark. "I...want a love that will last a lifetime. I don't think Grace believes there's such a thing."

"Then you need to convince her there is."

They'd reached the lower slopes where the topography leveled out. In winter, these were the nursery slopes where beginners learned to ski. Jack started to jog. He was keen to get to work, and in spite of himself, he couldn't wait to see Grace again.

He stopped at Matt's vehicle and leaned against it, waiting for his brother.

Matt took a few minutes to join him and another minute to catch his breath, then said, "I'm glad...I parked here and not in town. I can't manage...another step."

"Take a look at how much you've achieved today," Jack said, indicating the mountain.

They could spot the ridge they'd reached, high above them.

"I swear that mountain is way bigger than it was when we were kids," Matt said.

Jack patted his back. "Nope, still exactly two miles above sea level to the ridge. Another half mile of elevation to the top of Sourdough. We'll be hiking to the peak by the end of next week."

"That's a relief. I was afraid you were going to say we'd be hiking to the peak tomorrow."

"Just think of all those doughnuts you'll be able to eat when you do that."

"After all that exertion, the thought of doughnuts makes me feel sick."

Jack laughed and Matt opened his car door, apparently in no mood to share his amusement.

"Want a lift back into town?"

"Nope. I need to clear my head. See you same time tomorrow. And park your vehicle another two hundred yards down the hill. You need the extra exercise."

Matt grunted. "See you tomorrow," he said, and drove off in the direction of his office.

Jack stuck his hands in his pockets and strolled into town. Since the hike hadn't taken as long as he'd expected, he'd get to the job site before anyone else arrived. He pushed the door open into Rusty's and ordered coffee and granola.

"Nice group of kids you've got working for you, Jack," Rusty said as he plunked the coffeepot on the counter, leaving Jack to refill his cup as often as he wanted.

Jack poured the coffee, added milk and took a mouthful. His eyes closed in bliss. Nothing beat Rusty's coffee.

"Thanks. They're keen to learn and they work hard. Haven't had a lick of trouble with any of them. Did they enjoy their meal last night?"

"Very much. Here's the bill," Rusty said. Jack didn't bother to check it, just pulled out his wallet, peeled off some twenties and said, "Hope this covers it."

Rusty took the money, glanced at the bill and said, "Sure does." He dropped some of the cash into the tip jar. "How come you never check the bill? Those kids could be ordering caviar for all you know."

"You don't serve caviar in this dive. I trust the kids to be sensible, and since you won't serve them alcohol, we don't have a problem. Most of these kids have been treated pretty badly by adults all their lives. I figure extending them some trust and hoping they don't abuse it can't hurt."

Rusty nodded. "One of them, Tyrone, was asking if I had any evening work for him."

"He's a good kid. Not sure he's had any waiter experience, though."

"He's happy to start as a dishwasher. And he sounds more interested in short-order cooking than in waiting tables."

Jack finished his bowl of granola but was still hungry. The early-morning hike had left him with an appetite. He picked up the breakfast menu.

"Tyrone won't have any references, but you can use me, if you want. The kid is a hard worker and, in my opinion, honest. Just don't work him too hard so he's useless to me the next day."

"I'll give him two nights a week, Friday and Saturday, if that's okay with you? He has all of Sunday to recover," Rusty said, and grinned. "What else can I get you?"

"Ham and poached eggs on an English muffin, thanks."

Rusty took the order through to the kitchen and returned to where Jack sat. "So who was the pretty lady sittin' with you yesterday?"

"I thought you were cooking yesterday," Jack hedged.

"Was. Just 'cause I'm in the kitchen doesn't mean I can't keep an eye on the place. So, who is she?"

"She's contracted me to restore Missy Saunders's old place."

"So that's Grace Saunders?" Rusty asked. "She sure has grown up some. Didn't you two date in high school?"

Jack had forgotten that Rusty had opened his bar and grill while Jack was still in school. He'd had a soda fountain back then, too. Jack and Grace had spent more than a few afternoons there.

"I'd rather not talk about it, if you don't mind," Jack said, refilling his mug and moving to a booth—away from the bar so he wouldn't have to endure any more questions. Rusty was a great guy, but being a local bar owner, he knew and passed on a lot of gossip.

"I'll take my eggs over here," Jack said, grabbing a copy of the newspaper and indicating he needed space to read it as he slipped into a booth. Fortunately, the place started to fill with patrons and Jack didn't see Rusty until he placed the plate of ham and eggs in front of him.

"Enjoy," Rusty said, and disappeared into the kitchen.

Jack decided he'd eat breakfast at Maria's café in future. Maria could be every bit as nosy as Rusty, but since she didn't start her shift until the children were at school, he'd miss having her stop by the table to interrogate him.

A HALF HOUR LATER and stuffed with food and coffee, Jack turned in at the gate.

Al's truck was already parked out front. "Morning, boss," Tyrone greeted him as he mounted the front steps. "What do you want me to do today?"

"Morning, Tyrone. I hear you're looking for some work at Rusty's?"

Tyrone's normally open expression grew a little

alarmed. "You don't mind, do you? I wanted to save for a car. There are some real bargains in the paper," he said.

"No, I don't mind at all, Tyrone. I admire your initiative. But run it by Judge O'Malley first. And before you buy a car, let me know and we'll go check it out together. I'll have a local mechanic make sure you don't buy a lemon."

Tyrone's face split into a huge grin. "Thanks, boss. Man…you're somethin' special. You know that?"

Jack clapped him on the back. "You're a hard worker, Tyrone. I admire that in a person, so I'm happy to help out. How about if you go and ask Al what he wants you to start on today?"

Tyrone nodded and disappeared inside.

"That was a nice thing for you to do."

Jack spun around. Grace was leaning against the railing. He'd been so involved with Tyrone, he hadn't even noticed her arrival. He took in her outfit. She wasn't wearing overalls, but she was at least better covered than yesterday. A shirt unbuttoned over a scoop-neck T-shirt, jeans and the steel-toed boots. The tight-fitting jeans *could* have left a little more to the imagination. But he'd get her working so hard today, Grace might regret not wearing something more loose-fitting and comfortable.

"He's a good kid," he finally answered. "I'll go out of my way for anyone who wants to get ahead in life."

Grace climbed the stairs and came to stand right in front of him. "I hear you go out of your way for a lot of people."

"You don't want to believe everything you hear in this town."

"Not even from Mrs. Carmichael, the florist?"

"When did you meet her?"

"I stopped by to get some flowers to cheer up my hotel room. We got to chatting. Seems she's a big admirer of your family, especially your brother Will, in spite of his friendship with her husband's pig."

Jack laughed. Will and Louella and their strange friendship was a source of amusement and sometimes consternation around town.

"Don't be surprised if he stops by here one day with Louella tagging along. They hang out when he's in town. Otherwise, she gets up to mischief, and then Mayor Farquar gets into trouble with Becky."

Grace held up her hands. "Whoa there, go back a couple of steps. Why does the mayor get into trouble with Becky?"

"The mayor is Mrs. C.'s husband and he owns Louella. He and Becky don't exactly see eye to eye on pigs living inside the town limits. Mrs. Carmichael kept her former married name because no one could get used to calling her Mrs. Farquar."

Grace shook her head. "I'm still not sure I understand all that. But I look forward to meeting Louella. I think." She frowned and Jack wanted to smooth out the line with his finger.

"Anyway, I have good news. I've found somewhere to stay in town," she said. "Speaking of Mrs. Carmichael...I've taken the apartment over her shop. In fact, I've moved in already."

No wonder he hadn't heard her car pull up. Grace must have walked the two blocks to the house.

"You should've called me. I'd have helped you move your stuff."

"Not much to move. I do have a favor to ask, however."

"Done," Jack said without waiting to hear what it was.

"I'm returning my rental and so I'll need a ride back from Silver Springs later today, if that's convenient for you?"

"Won't you want a vehicle to get around?"

Grace shrugged. "I can walk anywhere I need to go in town."

Chapter Ten

Jack finished the day by ordering more lumber. Designers from two firms that hand-built custom-fit kitchens had come by, and Marcie Mason and Grace had spent a long time with them. So long that they'd both missed lunch.

Jack offered to order some sandwiches to be delivered from Rusty's, but Marcie had to go to another meeting soon after the rest of Jack's team had departed for the day. That left Jack and Grace sitting on the front porch, sharing the remains of Jack's lunch—the one he'd been too busy to eat himself.

"I can't believe the progress that's been made already," Grace remarked, and bit into a ham-and-cheese sandwich.

"Some weeks you won't notice any difference. Then you'll be nagging me to get a move on."

"I do not nag!" Grace protested.

Jack grinned. He enjoyed getting under Grace's skin. "Let's make a bet. If you haven't nagged by the time this renovation is finished, I'll owe you one hundred dollars. You nag and you have to pay up. *Every* time you nag."

"That's hardly fair! You'd only have to pay once, while I could be digging into my purse plenty of times."

"I thought you said you didn't nag."

Grace glowered. He had her there, but she was determined to win. "Deal?"

"Deal," he said, and they shook on it.

As he released her hand, she caught his in both of hers, turned it over and said as she examined his arm, "Your eczema has really responded to the cream and your new diet." Then she rubbed her forefinger over the calluses on his hand.

Jack swallowed, half embarrassed, half turned on by her attention as she continued to rub her fingers over the badge of his profession. Finally he could take it no longer and cleared his throat.

Grace snapped out of her trance and released him. "Sorry. I couldn't help noticing your calluses."

"I work with my hands, Grace. They're unavoidable."

She smiled and it melted his heart. "There's something incredibly sexy about a man who works with his hands." She shrugged. "It's masculine, I guess."

"And men without calluses aren't masculine?"

"My ex had a weekly manicure. I always felt there was something weirdly effeminate about that."

Jack smiled. Grace had been a nail-biter. It was one of the many things he'd loved about her. The insecurity it spoke of made him feel protective toward her.

"Trust me, you'll want to have short nails when you're using power tools or sanding what seems like acres of wood or stripping wallpaper."

"I can hardly wait," she said drolly.

"I won't be around much tomorrow. I've got a lot of ordering to do and I have to check Adam's site since I want to get the foundations laid this summer. Two of my guys have moved over to concreting and another to bricklaying. They've got jobs with other contractors in town, so they can all work on Adam's house while we work here. My brothers and I have always helped build one another's homes on the weekends. It brings us together and defuses some of the tension that builds up during the week at our jobs."

"Except that *you'll* be doing the same thing you do all week." Grace finished up her sandwich and placed the wrapper back in the paper bag. "That was delicious, by the way."

"Thanks, Tyrone made it. He's on lunch duty every day—gets up early and puts sandwiches and drinks together for all of us. I've added you to his list for tomorrow."

"I don't want to be any bother! I can grab something in town."

"Where you could get waylaid talking to someone or take too long over lunch. This way you're on-site and I can get the most out of you, workwise."

"Slave driver." She laughed, knowing Jack was joking.

"Sure am." Jack stood, took the package from her and neatly pitched it into a trash can on the porch.

"Do your apprentices all live in town?"

"Yes, in an old house on Main Street. They bunk together for free but each has a duty to attend to in lieu of rent. Tyrone's is making the lunches, Zac cleans and Ace does the gardening for all my properties."

"You own a number of properties?"

"Most in partnership with Will."

"And where do you live?" Grace asked as she stepped out the front gate ahead of Jack.

"In a miner's shack outside town."

"That doesn't sound very luxurious."

"It isn't. But it suits me. For now." He opened Betsy's passenger door. "We can return your car to the rental place now if you'd like."

GRACE CLIMBED IN. So Jack owned a "number" of properties in town? He'd done well for himself. And here she was, after all those years of studying and working, and all she owned was a run-down house she could never sell—and a condo in Boston with a huge mortgage. Since she'd been gullible enough to sign a prenup with Edward, she'd walked away from their marriage with her clothes, some savings and a couple of pieces of furniture she'd bought with her own money. That was it.

"Before I forget. Mom's issued an edict. I'm supposed to bring you to dinner this Friday. If you have something else to do, tell me now so I can let her down gently."

Grace didn't have anything planned for her evenings—for the rest of her life. But dinner with the O'Malleys might be too much, too soon.

"Uh, I was planning on attending one of the summertime concerts this Friday," Grace lied, and almost choked. She hated lying.

Jack started the truck and pulled into the street. He glanced across at her. "Then you should buy your ticket now, because saying you're 'planning' to do something and actually making a commitment by paying for it are two very different things to my mom."

Grace smiled. Jack's mom was a sweetheart. But she also could be a formidable woman…

"Maybe you could take me by the box office now and I can buy a ticket." Grace had no idea what was playing, but anything would be better than being confronted by the O'Malleys en masse.

Shostakovitch's Cello Concerto, Grace read in the Friday night performance program. Ugh! Cello music was so depressing. So not what she needed right now. She preferred lighthearted orchestral music.

"I can see by your face that you're not a fan."

"I wonder if there's anything more interesting happening in Denver. Like a baseball game," she said with as much enthusiasm as someone heading to the gallows.

Jack chuckled at her remark and pointed to the poster advertising upcoming recitals at the Spruce Lake performing Arts Center. "Saturday night is *Swan Lake,*" he said. "I bet you're a sucker for Tchaikovsky."

"I am," she said dreamily. "Oh, and next Saturday is Hits of Hollywood," she noted, looking farther down the program. "I wonder if I can get season tickets. I'll need some cultural diversion in this town."

"From what I recall, you were never a snob, Grace."

"I'm sorry. But I don't want to spend every night sitting alone in the apartment over Mrs. C.'s shop watching television or…knitting."

"You knit?"

"No, I don't. But it seems like something you'd do when you don't have anything else to occupy your time." She glanced up at him and confessed, "The truth is, Jack, that I adore your family but I know what they're like. The thought of them asking about our relationship fills me with panic."

Grinning, Jack said, "How about this—you come to dinner on Friday, thus saving yourself from falling asleep during the cello concerto, and I'll accompany you to *Swan Lake*."

"You'd do that?"

"Sure. I'm not a complete knucklehead, you know." Jack approached the box-office window. "Two of your best seats for Saturday night," he said to the attendant.

"No, let me pay!" Grace protested, trying to elbow him aside.

"Too late," Jack said, taking the tickets from the attendant and tapping Grace on the nose with them.

"My treat next time, then."

"We'll see," Jack said, and headed back to his truck, giving Grace no alternative but to follow.

A half hour later, they'd picked up and returned her rental and were back on the road to Spruce Lake. The sun was setting over the mountains, leaving the sky a glowing pink. Grace couldn't help sighing at the beauty of it.

"I have an even better view of the sunsets from my shack," Jack said. "You'll have to come see it sometime."

Chapter Eleven

"Grace?"

Grace looked up from sanding the front railings to find a woman with dark red hair and vivid green eyes mounting the steps onto the veranda. The woman held out her hand and said, "I'm Becky O'Malley, Jack's sister-in-law."

Feeling less than presentable, Grace wiped her dusty palm on her jeans, took Becky's hand and shook it. "Jack just went to the hardware store."

"Actually, I'm looking for you. I'm on my lunch break from the courthouse and I like to take a walk to clear my head before the afternoon session." Becky rested her hip against the railing and crossed her arms. "Looks like Jack gave you one of the rotten jobs," she said, indicating the sandpaper Grace was holding.

Grace made a face. "I can tell you, it's getting old fast. I've decided I'm going to pay one of the guys extra to do this job for me. Come on inside."

Becky followed her into the house and let out a low whistle. "Wow, what a mess!"

"I'm already having serious doubts about this project," Grace admitted as she washed her hands at the sink, the only part of the counter Ace had left in his demolition of the kitchen.

"I'm sure it'll all be worth it in the end," Becky told her. "What have you planned for the house?"

Grace took her on a tour of the main floor and then they headed upstairs. Becky nodded her approval throughout, and once they'd reached the old bathroom, she sat on the edge of the bath and indicated Grace should join her.

"So, tell me about you and Jack," she said.

Surprised by her forthrightness, Grace said, "There's nothing to tell. He's renovating the house for me."

"And then?"

"Then I'll have to find someone to rent it. I'm sort of bound by trust to keep it in the family."

"Would you consider staying and living in it yourself?"

"And where would I work?"

"We need more doctors in this town. Especially good doctors. Female doctors."

"I'm a pediatrician. I doubt there are enough children here for a busy practice."

"You'd be surprised. There isn't a pediatrician between here and Denver. You'd be in huge demand."

Suspicious, Grace couldn't help asking, "Why are you pushing the point? You hardly know me."

"Truthfully? I want to see Jack happy."

"I don't see what that's got to do with me."

"He was in love with you once. I think he still is."

Startled by Becky's remark, Grace said, "Jack and I were just high school sweethearts—a long time ago."

"Jack mentioned that you were married when you lived in Boston."

Grace screwed up her face. "Worst ten years of my life. And that's saying something!"

"He said you had a pretty lousy childhood. Me, too. And a lousier marriage. I was determined that nothing and no one would touch my heart again. And then Will O'Malley roared into my courtroom and drove me to distraction with his antics over that pig of Frank Farquar's. And when *that* didn't work, he set his family on me and made my son fall in love with him. After that, I had no hope of resisting him."

Grace laughed at the tale and the way Becky told it, as if she was still half-mad at herself for letting Will get under her skin so easily.

"It might have worked for you, Becky, but I have no intention of ever marrying again."

"I felt like that, too." Becky shrugged. "However, we're all different. I just don't want to see my brother-in-law pining his life away."

"And now you're being overdramatic!"

Becky laughed. "Okay—"

Tyrone burst into the bathroom and stopped in his tracks. "Sorry, Ms. Saunders. Judge. I didn't know anyone was in here."

"Anything we can do for you, Tyrone?" Grace asked the boy. She was fond of Tyrone. He was a hard worker who had a cheerful nature and a cheeky smile.

"I'm s'posed to start demolishing the bathroom. Ace is on his way over to show me how."

He turned to Becky. "Jack said I should come talk

to you about a job I want to take at Rusty's on Friday and Saturday nights."

Becky nodded. "He told me about it already and I'm pleased you want to work and save. How about if you come and see me at the courthouse when you knock off here tonight and we'll go over it? Just tell them I'm expecting you."

"Thanks, Judge," he said, and then looked uncomfortable. "Sorry, ma'am, Judge, I'll have to ask you to move so Ace and I can get the bathtub out."

The bathroom was yet another seventies renovation nightmare. There wasn't anything in it worth preserving, so Grace had agreed that Ace should demolish it the way he'd done the kitchen.

Ace appeared then, brandishing a sledgehammer, and she and Becky squeezed past him. "Water's turned off," he said to Tyrone. "Let's get to work."

Becky and Grace went down to the first floor, accompanied by the sounds of smashing tiles.

Jack had returned from the hardware store. "Guess I better order another Dumpster," he said, glancing up the stairs toward the racket. "I'm not sure Ace is cut out to be a carpenter, but he has a real talent for demolition."

"Is there any danger he'll accidentally demolish the whole house?" Grace asked mock seriously.

"He might," Jack said, then couldn't keep a straight face.

Becky laughed, too. "I spoke to Tyrone about the job at Rusty's. He's going to see me after work."

"I suspect the reason you just happened to come by has nothing to do with Tyrone," Jack said.

"Just wanted to meet Spruce Lake's newest resident."

Jack looked at Grace and said, deadpan, "You've met the nosiest of my sisters-in-law. The rest are pussycats compared to Becky."

Becky punched him lightly on the arm.

Grace watched the exchange, seeing the genuine affection between them. "Then I can't wait to meet them," she said, and turned to Becky. "It was a pleasure talking to you, Becky, and I look forward to seeing you on Friday night."

"You're coming to dinner?"

"If your sisters-in-law are half as nice as you, I wouldn't miss it."

Becky's face glowed. "Sarah will be delighted. She speaks highly of you."

"You've discussed me?" Grace was starting to feel uncomfortable.

"It's the real reason I dropped by. To make sure Jack remembered to invite you."

"Which I already have and she's accepted."

"Then tell your mom, will you?" Becky said, a bit flustered. "Otherwise, you'll have a never-ending stream of O'Malley women showing up to meet Grace and talk her into coming to dinner."

Jack pulled out his cell and turned away to make a call. "Mom, stop siccing the girls on Grace, okay? She's coming on Friday."

Becky checked her watch. "I'd better go back to the madhouse," she said. "Let's do lunch sometime soon, okay? I job-share with another judge, so I work two days one week and three the following. Unless we have a big case, and then I have to stay for the duration. But it would be great to get together with you, Grace. Just us girls. I'll call Beth, Carly and Megan and have them clear their schedules."

"SHE WASN'T TOO PUSHY, was she?" Jack asked after Becky had left.

"No, of course not," Grace assured him. "In fact, I found her charming. I gather you two work together with some of your apprentices?"

Jack nodded. "I have a friend who's a social worker in L.A. He lets me know about kids who might benefit from being around some positive male role models and getting away from the city and the bad influences there. Matt has contacts in Denver and Miami who do the same. The kids meet with Becky every week to talk about how they're doing, what they want to do with their lives, stuff like that. Some of them come in as real hard cases, but a half hour with Becky pretty much beats the attitude out of them and they're willing to do anything to get away from her."

Grace laughed and said, "That's a bit unfair. Tyrone seems to like her."

"Becky doesn't care if the kids *like* her. The point is, Tyrone *respects* her. He was one of the worst cases when he arrived. He's made huge improvements in his life and I'm glad to see he's taking the initiative of applying for another job. It's the best I can hope for, that they become financially independent and are happy in their chosen careers, whatever those might be. But if Tyrone works out at Rusty's I could be looking for another apprentice."

"And someone to make the lunches."

A crash echoed from above, followed by masculine bellows of laughter. "I'd better go check that out," he said.

As Jack took the stairs two at a time, Grace watched, enjoying his fluid movements.

So, tomorrow night she'd be having dinner at Two Elk. Just like old times. Well, not quite the same, since the family had been added to significantly in the intervening years.

What they didn't know was that there was another member of the family out there, one they'd never meet.

Chapter Twelve

"You can't pay Tyrone extra to do a job he's supposed to do, anyway," Jack said.

"I was paying him extra to do *my* job!" Grace explained. "All that sanding was killing my hands. Plus, it's boring."

"What happened to you helping out with the renovation?"

"I'm helping! I'm just giving the guy some extra cash to do the dull bits. Anyway, you and I both know I don't have to do any of this if I don't want to. *I'm* the one paying the bills. Stop being so high-handed."

Unmoved, Jack crossed his arms and said, "Then we'll have to find a job that doesn't involve getting your precious hands dirty."

"I'm good at picking paint colors."

"Which takes all of ten minutes."

"Um, sweeping?"

"I heard you offering to pay Ace to do that."

"The broom gave me splinters!"

"Then wear gloves."

"It's too hot to wear gloves!"

"This sounds a lot like nagging to me. Pretty soon you'll have to make good on our bet."

"The hell I will!" Grace protested.

AFTER ASKING JACK what to wear to Friday dinner and being told "country casual," Grace went back to Perkins Clothing and Boots, the store where she'd bought her steel-toed boots.

The store was an interesting mix of Western fashion, footwear and even haberdashery, much like the stores of a hundred and fifty years earlier. Grace had noticed some nice denim skirts and checkered shirts when she'd bought her boots. As she walked inside, she was assailed by the scent of leather and something like old tobacco smoke. She made her way to ladies' apparel and hunted through the skirts, settling on one that reached her knees and another that was considerably shorter. She picked out some scoop-neck T-shirts, since Jack didn't seem able to keep his eyes off her cleavage when she wore them, and for modesty at the O'Malley dinner table, Grace also chose several checked cotton shirts. After trying the clothing on, she paid for her goods and left the store, feeling very pleased with herself.

She bumped into Becky and a young teenage boy on their way into Perkins. "Grace!" Becky said. "What are *you* looking so smug about?"

Grace held up the packages and stopped herself from blurting, "Step one accomplished in the seduction of Jack O'Malley," and said instead, "Successful shopping trip for an outfit for tomorrow night's dinner." She glanced at the boy and held out her hand. "Hi, you must be Becky's son. I'm Grace."

The boy grinned, his freckles nearly joining up as he shook Grace's hand. "Nick. Mom's making me get clothes here. She thinks I've grown out of everything. I'd rather shop in Denver." He rolled his eyes.

Laughing, Grace said, "When I was a kid, I used to feel exactly the same way about shopping here in town. Now, I'm more than happy with what I found."

"What did you get?" Becky asked, trying to peek into the bags.

"You'll see tomorrow," Grace said, holding them away from her. "Meanwhile, I need a manicure. I have yet to meet your sisters-in-law and I don't want them thinking I'm a slob."

"Trust me, they won't. Each of us had to learn that life in the mountains—especially life with the O'Malleys— isn't about appearances, but about heart. And they've all got plenty of that."

"Still…I'd feel better if my hands looked a little nicer."

Becky smiled and said, "Then go and see Patty and tell her I sent you. Her salon is above the craft store. Anyway, I need to buy some new jeans for this son of mine or he'll burst out of these standing here on the doorstep. I can't believe how fast he's growing!"

Being a pediatrician, Grace had heard that from mothers so many times. "Just be happy he's growing and healthy, Becky. Trust me, he'll slow down one day, although don't expect that until he's almost out of his teens."

"He's just turned thirteen!" Becky protested. "Maybe they sell jeans I can get taken down." she muttered under her breath.

"Mom!"

"Oh, all right," Becky said, "I was only trying to economize. See you tomorrow, Grace, if not before." She waved as she stepped through the door Nick was holding open for her.

Smiling, Grace wandered down Main Street toward the manicurist Becky had recommended. She doubted she'd get an appointment this late in the day, but she could always sneak out tomorrow.

"Gracie Saunders!"

Grace spun around to see who'd called her, and her heart sank. Letitia Malone. She'd know that supercilious look anywhere. Lettie had been one of the girls who'd teased Grace about her hand-me-down clothes in high school. Grace had hoped she'd run into Letitia the day she'd arrived, driving a European sports car and wearing her Christian Louboutin pumps. Instead, here she was, dressed in dusty jeans and steel-toed boots.

"Letitia. You're still living here?" she said in a voice meant to convey that Letitia hadn't done much with her life if she still lived in the same town she grew up in.

"Yeah, I'm married with five kids. You?"

"Oh, I live in Boston now. I'm a pediatrician."

Letitia smirked. "You're a foot doctor?"

It took Grace a moment to realize what Lettie was talking about. "No. A *pediatrician* looks after kids," she explained patiently. Lettie had never been the smartest girl in class. She made up for it by being the meanest.

"So, how old are your kids?" she asked.

"Thirteen, eleven, seven, four and two." Lettie patted her stomach. "I'm pregnant again," she crowed, clearly proud of her reproductive powers.

So Lettie had gotten pregnant right out of high school. "And your husband? Did you marry someone local?"

"'Course. Jamie Whitaker," Lettie said smugly.

Jamie. The football jock. He'd been popular with the girls, but never particularly discriminating. He'd tried to hit on Grace once, but she'd just given him a look and walked away. It had been a mistake, because then he'd spread the rumor that she'd slept with him. The in crowd had believed Jamie, although no one else did. But it had hurt, and Jack had gotten into a fight with him. Jack had lost. Grace winced at the memory. It was one of the many unhappy incidents of her school life she'd endeavored to overcome. The fact that she was standing in the middle of Main Street reliving the experience was proof she hadn't been entirely successful.

Wanting to get away from Lettie and the memories, she said, "I'm so glad it all worked out for you, Lettie. You and Jamie deserve each other. Now, if you'll excuse me, I have an appointment." She turned away, hating her bitchy tone but nevertheless triumphant at the shock on Lettie's face.

"Yeah, well, just make sure you keep away from him!" Lettie shouted to her back.

"That won't be a problem," Grace muttered under her breath. "Damn!" she said, angry that she hadn't been dressed to the nines when she'd run into Lettie. It shouldn't matter what some skank from her past thought of her, but Grace had wanted to show at least one of the girls who'd been so mean to her how successful she'd become.

Successful! Ha! What a joke. She had money and

nice clothes and a prestigious career. But "Loosie Lettie" had the kids and the husband. Grace had no idea why that annoyed her so much. After all, who in her right mind would want to be married to Jamie Whitaker? *And* have his kids!

Flustered, Grace missed the manicurist's shop and had to double back. She dreaded bumping into Lettie again. The woman had made her feel so uncomfortable that all Grace wanted to do was flee, get out of Spruce Lake and away from the bad memories.

"Hey! What's biting your butt?"

Grace met Matt's concerned eyes. "You okay, Grace? You look like you want to punch something," he said.

Grace took several deep breaths, trying to compose herself. "Hi, Matt. I'm sorry." She shrugged. "I just ran headlong into my past and I didn't enjoy it."

"Care to discuss?"

"It's only stupid teenage angst."

Matt crossed his arms. "Which you're apparently still dealing with."

"You got that right," she said, and shook her head. "I shouldn't have come here thinking I could…"

"Could what?"

Matt was too astute, which probably made him a good cop, but she was too wound up to talk.

She shook her head. "Nothing. I…need to go."

"Why don't we grab a soda?"

Grace knew Matt wasn't going to take no for an answer. "Shouldn't you be out hunting down criminals?"

"If you told me who upset you, I could go hunt them down and arrest them." He caught her elbow and steered Grace into the café they were standing in front of. Grace collapsed into a chair and Matt sat opposite her, resting his big arms on the table. The waitress arrived with two glasses of water. Matt ordered his diet soda, while Grace asked for a pot of herbal tea. Tea always helped calm her nerves.

"What's the statute of limitations on bullying?" she asked Matt, half hoping it was twenty-five years.

Matt frowned. "Someone bullied you in the street?"

"No, it goes way back. To high school. I ran into someone who used to make my life a living hell."

Matt nodded. "Lettie Malone."

"How'd you guess?"

"She's one of the few girls from that group who stayed in the district. She married that no-hope football jock, Jamie Whitaker. I know what he said about you, Grace, and it was so unfair. We all knew it was blatantly untrue. I remember Jack came home with a black eye and bloodied nose."

Jack, her hero, had tried to protect her honor and had suffered for it.

"Being bullied at school can affect people for the rest of their lives," Matt said. "If it's any consolation, Jamie got his comeuppance. He got Lettie pregnant. Lettie's father brought out the shotgun and they had a quickie wedding. That pretty much spelled the end of his football career." Matt shook his head. "He had so much talent and threw it away. What an idiot."

Grace was taken aback. She hadn't expected Matt to be this critical of someone.

"Yet they're still married," Grace said.

"She tell you that?"

"Not in so many words. Did I get that wrong?"

"Jamie plays around. They keep separating but she keeps taking him back. Or forcing him to come back by getting pregnant to 'save' the marriage."

Grace had no time for women who clung to men who cheated on them. Thank goodness Edward hadn't been a cheat—just a controlling jerk. "How pathetic of her. I do feel sorry for the children, though."

"Me, too. As expected, they're turning out pretty much like their parents. The oldest boy's been in court on shoplifting charges. The oldest girl is boy-crazy and headed for a teen pregnancy if she doesn't smarten up."

"Not much chance any of them will smarten up with parents like that."

Matt smiled and said, "'Atta girl. Lettie and Jamie covered their stupidity in high school with bullying and lies. Unfortunately, intelligence has nothing to do with fertility."

"Ain't that the truth. In my practice—" Grace cut herself off, not wanting to talk about Boston or her career. And especially not about Lettie and Jamie and their kids.

"You were going to say?"

Grace waved his comment away. "Let's talk about *your* family. A much nicer subject! Fill me in on who's married to whom and what the children's names are so I'm prepared tomorrow night."

Matt spent the next fifteen minutes doing just that, sharing anecdotes and making Grace feel more at ease about meeting them all. Now they didn't seem like such a horde of strangers. "I've met Nick already. He was going shopping with Becky," she said.

Matt grinned. "She bemoans the way that kid's growing, but secretly, I think she's damned proud he *is* growing."

"Something the matter with him?"

"You didn't notice his limp?"

"No. We bumped into one another in the shop doorway. Why does he have a limp?"

"Cerebral palsy. His father ran out on them pretty soon after his birth. Becky raised him on her own and held her career together. She was so determined she could do it all, didn't need another man in her life. And then she met my brother."

"And they've lived happily ever after since," Grace finished.

"Not quite as simple as that. Becky wasn't easy to convince. Will had to pull out all the stops to show her they were meant to be together."

Grace nodded. "Becky did mention that Will made Nick fall in love with him before she did."

"Nick was a pushover. He was a great little guy and so starved for male attention. Will didn't know he was Becky's son for ages. Not until it was too late—for Becky. I must say, I learned true respect for my former ski bum of a brother because of the way he treated Nick. He taught him to swim and how to deal with bullies. That kid just blossomed under Will's care."

"If Will could convince Becky to marry him and make it work, it proves there's someone out there for all of us."

Grace looked up as a dark-haired man entered the café. He had a two-year-old girl perched on his hip and he seemed flustered. "That *is* Will, isn't it?" she asked, suddenly unsure which O'Malley man she'd identified.

But she was sure of one thing—he was definitely an O'Malley.

Matt turned in his seat and Grace saw the brothers notice each other at the same time. Will smiled at Grace and said to Matt, "You seen my wife?"

"And hello to you, too," Matt said, taking the toddler from Will's arms. She went happily and he kissed the top of her head, then settled her on his lap. "Will, you remember Grace Saunders, don't you?"

"Sorry, yes. Hi, Grace. How are you managing with my brother?"

"Matt? He's a peach."

The little girl pulled at her ear and scowled.

"Matt? A peach?" He laughed and said, "That's an oxymoron if I ever heard one. No, I meant Jack. Becky said he makes you wear ugly clothes and cut your nails. Shocking. Just shocking." He shook his head to add dramatic emphasis.

Grace laughed at his melodrama. "Yes, he has. And I saw Becky not more than twenty minutes ago going into Perkins Clothing and Boots."

"She have Nick with her?"

"Yes."

"Poor kid."

"Poor kid?"

"Yeah, no teen would choose to buy clothes in a place that's been an institution for thousands of years. Especially not with his mother. He wanted jeans from a chain store. Becky wanted quality. I was supposed to meet him and take him shopping in Silver Springs before Becky could get hold of him."

The toddler started to cry and pulled her ear some more.

"How long has your little girl been doing that?" Grace asked.

"All day. She hasn't cried until now," he said, retrieving his daughter from Matt and patting her back to comfort her.

Grace felt the child's forehead. It was warm and sweaty, and the little girl didn't look happy at all. "Has she had a cold or runny nose lately?"

"How did you know?"

"She probably has an ear infection. I think you should go to the local doctor and have her checked out."

"I'm not taking her to Doc Jenkins! He should've retired years ago. I'll run her down to the hospital in the morning. Lucy Cochrane can take a look at her."

"By tomorrow she might have—"

"Might have what?"

Grace, Will and Matt hadn't noticed that Becky and Nick had entered the café.

Will told his wife, "Grace figures Lily's got an ear infection and I should get her to a doctor immediately."

"Not that fool Jenkins!" Becky said, reiterating what half the O'Malleys seemed to think of the town's doctor.

"I'll take Lily to the hospital right away," Will said, cradling his now-fractious daughter.

"There's no need to upset her with a long drive to the hospital. I can take a look at her if you like and prescribe something," Grace offered.

"Please!" Becky almost cried.

Grace was surprised by the panic in Becky's voice, but given that Nick, with his cerebral palsy, probably didn't always enjoy good health, it was understandable.

Grace moved over so Will could sit beside her in the booth. "Do you have a flashlight, Matt?" she asked.

He produced a small but powerful model and Grace cooed at Lily to settle her, then looked in her ear.

"Hoo, boy, that is one red eardrum. You're a brave little girl, Lily, for not making much of a fuss about it until now," she told the child with a smile, trying to ease any discomfort caused by a strange woman looking in her ear. Grace distracted Lily further by letting her play with the still-lit flashlight as she felt the glands in the child's neck.

"She needs acetaminophen and antibiotics. I don't have a prescription pad, but I'm happy to come to the pharmacy with you to get those before the infection turns really nasty."

"Thank you," Will said. "I feel terrible that I didn't do anything about it earlier. I thought she'd discovered her ear and decided it was something she wanted to play with."

"Perfectly reasonable," Grace said. "We'll have you back to your old self in no time, won't we, sweetie?" she asked Lily, then handed her to her father.

"Why don't you and I take Lily to the pharmacy, Grace," Becky suggested. "And Will can take Nicolas shopping for jeans in Silver Springs." She glowered at Nick, who glowered back. "Our son has turned into an argumentative teenager," she told her husband. "He absolutely refused to try on the jeans I'd picked out for him at Perkins."

Will slid out of the booth, allowing Grace to follow. Matt plunked a twenty on the table and said, "You want me to come, too? I could put on my lights and siren."

"Very funny," Becky said, and bustled out of the café, Grace on her heels, leaving the men to deal with the defiant teenager.

FRIDAY EVENING, GRACE washed and blow-dried her hair, then took a ridiculous amount of time with her makeup—ridiculous because she was trying for a natural look and that always seemed to take twice as long.

She was standing at the bathroom mirror, dressed only in the longer of her new denim skirts and her bra, when the doorbell rang.

"Coming!" she cried as she hurried into the bedroom and pulled on a camisole. Grabbing the red-and-white-checked shirt she'd chosen, Grace raced toward the front door. Except she collided with Jack's broad chest.

"Whoa!" He caught her arms to stop her from falling backward. "Where are you going in such a rush?"

"To answer the door. The door you're supposed to be waiting on the other side of."

"You said, 'Come in.'"

"No. I said, 'Coming!'"

Jack shrugged and blatantly studied her outfit. His scrutiny made her face warm—followed by the rest of her body as his gaze fell to her bare legs. "Door was unlocked. Sorry."

"Damn!" Grace said as she slipped on sandals. "Mrs. C. told me to be careful of the door. It comes off its latch, then won't lock."

Jack strode to the door, inspected it and said, "I'll be back in a second."

Grace used the time to finish putting on her lipstick and checking herself in the mirror. Deciding that Jack hadn't reacted quite enough to the skirt, she changed into the shorter one. Grace wanted his gaze lingering on her legs. She then buttoned the shirt that was just a little too snug and went back into the living room to find Jack on his knees, working on her door lock. She walked right up to him, so his eyes were level with the hem of her skirt, and said, "Everything okay?"

Jack turned and she was pleased to see him swallow. "Fine. I'll be done in a minute," he said gruffly.

"Would you like a drink before we go?"

"I'm driving," he said, and stood. "That's done. Anything else need fixing while I'm here?"

Grace poured two tall glasses of iced tea, then sat on the sofa and patted the spot beside her. "We're a few minutes early. Come sit down and relax."

Jack went to the kitchen faucet, where he washed and dried his hands, before joining her. Grace handed him his drink, then clinked her glass with his. "To old times," she said.

Jack looked into her eyes. "What are you trying to do to me, Grace?"

"Do?"

"You've changed your skirt."

"Is it too short for tonight?" she asked, wide-eyed. She was prepared to change if Jack thought it was too risqué for the O'Malley dinner table, but in the meantime, she had every intention of showing Jack as much skin as possible.

She crossed one leg over the other and leaned toward him, waiting for his answer.

"It's fine, Grace. I just want to know why you changed."

"Why do you think?" she asked, placing a fingernail against his chest.

Jack sucked in a breath, caught her hand and put his drink on the coffee table. Then he took Grace's glass and set it beside his. He turned to Grace, clasped her face in his hands and kissed her.

Now this is more like it, Grace thought, returning the kiss as she clasped his shirtfront in her fingers and drew him closer.

Jack broke the kiss slowly and touched his finger to the end of her nose, saying, "That's all for now. We're late." He reached for her hand and drew her to her feet.

Grace stood, feeling slightly off balance and hoping the evening at the ranch passed quickly, so they could return to her apartment and continue where they'd left off.

Chapter Thirteen

"I feel strangely nervous about seeing your parents again and meeting the rest of your family," Grace admitted as they headed out of town toward Two Elk.

"Don't be. Mom can't wait to see you. You already know my brothers and most of my sisters-in-law. Plus, you're already a big hit for diagnosing Lily's ear infection," Jack assured her.

Still, Grace fretted most of the way. When they pulled up outside the ranch house, the front door flew open and Sarah O'Malley rushed outside.

Grace hopped down from the truck and was enfolded in Sarah's arms. "I'm so happy to see you again, Grace," she said. "It's been far too long. Come on into the house."

Relieved that Sarah held no ill will toward her for leaving Spruce Lake, Grace reached back into the truck's cab and retrieved the flowers she'd brought for Sarah. "Thank you for inviting me, Mrs. O'Malley," she said. "I hope you can do something with these."

"Why, thank you, dear. And you're way too old to be calling me Mrs. O'Malley," she said. "It's Sarah, and Mr. O'Malley will insist on being called Mac."

"There she is!" Will said, coming out into the yard.

Lily was on his hip, looking a lot happier than she had the previous day.

Before they climbed the porch steps, Grace was sure she'd been greeted by most of the O'Malleys and met most of their children.

Her earlier nervousness soon disappeared and she felt like one of the family again—as she had all those years ago. Only then, she hadn't appreciated it as much as she should've. Everyone made their way into the kitchen, where the children resumed their seats to finish their supper.

"There are so many of us now, Grace," Sarah explained. "We need two dinner sittings. It feels like a cruise ship." She laughed and then went to help one of the kids.

Although she was a pediatrician, Grace didn't always feel like a natural around children. However, the O'Malley tribe were polite and seemed to have good appetites. No one was whining about their meal and no one was throwing food at anyone else. Then again, having a grandmother like Sarah, they wouldn't dare!

"You go on out back with the boys and watch the sunset," Sarah said. "Carly, Beth and I will be right with you."

"You sure you aren't doing too much, Mom?" Jack asked. "Will and Matt should be doing their share of dinner patrol."

"Lily's finished, so Will's putting her to bed." Sarah dished out plates of fruit salad and ice cream, then wiped her hands on her apron. "Go!" She shooed Jack and Grace outside.

As she stepped onto the back porch, Grace caught

her breath at the beauty of the sunset behind the mountains. The sky glowed with pinks, reds and oranges set against the deep blue sky higher up. She had a view of the sunset from her apartment in town, but it was nothing compared to this.

"Come take a seat and enjoy the serenity, Grace," Mac O'Malley said, indicating an Adirondack chair facing the mountains.

It was a beautiful summer evening. Crickets chirruped in the garden and farther away she could hear the occasional whinny of a horse and the lowing of the cattle on the slopes. Between the mountain that sat so majestically behind the property and the house was a huge lake. Grace remembered the fall colors of the aspen groves dotted around the lake. She'd once thought the location was heaven on earth. And if she was honest with herself, she didn't feel any differently now.

Jack sat down beside her and silently offered her a glass of white wine, and she smiled at him. They'd often sat out here and just enjoyed each other's company in the silence of the evening.

But the calm didn't last for long. Soon the yard was filled with O'Malley offspring. Their evening meal finished, they were ready to expend the last of their energy chasing one another around.

Sarah came out, a little girl perched on her hip. She handed Matt his daughter, who seemed to gauge the relaxed mood and placed her thumb in her mouth, closing her eyes.

The children tore around the yard like little hellions. One of them, a girl of about ten, tackled Nicolas to the ground. "Daisy!" Luke yelled a warning as if he was concerned his daughter could harm the much bigger boy. The pair both sat up, laughing. "I'm fine, Uncle Luke," Nick called.

An older girl was happy to find a vacant seat and join the adults. Grace wondered if this was Luke's oldest daughter, Sasha. Two younger girls chased each other but soon tired of their game. One went to sit on Luke's lap, the other on Adam's. Celeste and Maddy, Grace guessed. That would make the toddler in Matt's arms... Sarah! Pleased that she was managing without further input from Jack, she glanced around and whispered to him, "Where's Cody?"

"He'll be here shortly," Jack said.

Grace did a quick count of how many people lived in the ranch house. Before, it had been just the seven O'Malleys, Mac and Sarah and their five sons—although Luke and Matt had mostly been away at college when she and Jack were dating.

Now Luke had a wife and five children. Surely, with Mac and Sarah still living there, the house must be bursting at the seams. Noticing the extension built at a right angle to the house, she asked Jack, "Who lives there?" She whispered, not wanting to disturb the peace, but with the children's noise, she figured no one else would hear.

"Mom and Pop. Cody's moved into the apartment over the barn. It suffered smoke damage from a fire earlier this year, but my guys got the barn rebuilt and the apartment in order a month ago. As you can probably imagine, with four sisters, Cody loves having his own space."

"You had a fire?"

"Long story," he said. "No one was hurt and, thanks to Carly, all the horses were saved."

"I did not save all the horses!" Carly interrupted. "Just that nasty, ornery stallion of Luke's." She shuddered and rubbed her cheek. "I swear I can still feel where he kicked me."

"Good thing Luke let him roam the range and impregnate practically every mare out there. We'll have some strong foals next year," Mac said.

Mac wasn't known for chatting, and Grace didn't expect any further conversation from him. However, he seemed to want to talk. "You might like to come out for a ride with me sometime, Grace. Like we did in the old days."

Grace and Jack had often ridden with Jack's father to inspect the fences. She'd appreciated his quiet solitude, his capable way with animals. "I'd like that very much," she said.

"Dinner's ready!" Beth called from the back porch.

Since the sun had set behind the mountains now, the evening was turning chilly, as it often did in the high country. Eating outside wasn't an option, except on the warmest of nights.

The adults piled inside, some washing their hands at the sink, others disappearing to put toddlers to bed. The older children stayed outside to play.

Jack pulled out a chair for Grace, then took the seat beside her—just as he always had. Grace wondered how many women he'd brought home over the years to share a meal with the family. How many other lucky women had been made to feel a part of this large and boisterous clan?

Cody appeared and was introduced to Grace. The kid was an O'Malley through and through. With his dark hair and eyes, he was the image of his father and all his uncles except Jack, who shared his mother's blue eyes.

Food was passed around and conversation flowed. Now that it was dark outside, various children ran through the kitchen toward the living room and other parts of the house.

"So, Grace," Will said as he heaped more potatoes onto his plate, "when are you going to make an honest man outta my little brother?"

Conversation ceased and Grace could feel all eyes trained on her. Will was the most outspoken of his brothers, so the question wasn't completely out of left field, just inappropriate. She could feel Jack sitting stiffly beside her. Jack was the shiest of the brothers—even now—and she knew he'd be dying at Will's bluntness.

She took her time swallowing the mouthful that had become lodged in her throat, then picked up her glass of water, took several sips, and replaced it on the table. "I don't know, Will. Does your brother need to be made into an honest man?"

Mac grinned at her response and winked at her.

"He's the only one of us who hasn't managed to find a wife," Will said.

"He wouldn't be if I hadn't accepted that posting in this town and had you turn up in my court!" his wife, Becky, said. "Lord knows, no one else would be silly enough to fall for you!"

"True," Matt said, raising his glass. "We'd have two lovesick O'Malley bachelors if Becky hadn't agreed to marry you in a weak moment. I still can't wrap my head around how easily it happened, Will."

"It had absolutely nothing to do with him!" Becky protested. "Nicolas wanted a father, and Will was available."

Everyone laughed at that, except Will.

"You had that coming, little brother, for asking such a personal question," Luke said, and clapped him on the back as he refilled their glasses. Then he looked right at Grace and said, "So when *will* you make an honest man of my brother, Grace?"

"Since I don't think there's a more honest man in the county, your question, Will—and its follow-up, Luke— is irrelevant." She heard the soft exhalation of Jack's breath beside her.

"Well said!" Sarah said. "All of you, mind your own business. Jack and Grace's relationship is none of your concern."

"I'm so embarrassed," Jack muttered, just low enough for Grace to hear.

She turned her head slightly toward him and said, "Me, too."

"We can leave, if you want," he said a little louder, for the benefit of everyone else.

"What, and have an O'Malley man get the better of me? No way. Besides, I've seen what's for dessert and I'm not going anywhere until I've eaten my fill. It's been too many years since I've had a home-cooked meal."

"'Atta girl!" Mac said, and raised his glass to her.

"You don't cook?" Luke's wife, Megan, asked.

"I've never needed to. My hus—my *ex*-husband and I dined out a lot. If we ever ate at home, it was something from the freezer." Grace wished she'd just kept her mouth shut. *TMI!* she scolded herself. *Soon you'll be telling them that apart from evenings out at too many social functions, you and your ex rarely sat in the same room, let alone shared a meal.*

"I wish we ate out more," Will said, fully recovered from his mild chastisement. "My wife is a terrible cook."

This brought gales of laughter from everyone, including Becky.

"That's not entirely true. She makes great salads," Matt said, emptying the remains of the salad bowl onto his plate.

"And beautiful children!" Beth added.

Relieved that the focus was now off her relationship with Jack, Grace said, "Okay, tell me about Louella. I've been hearing all sorts of things about her, but nothing makes much sense."

"Which is entirely the point," Matt said. "Louella is Will's best friend. If you can make any sense of why a self-respecting pig would want to hang out with him in her spare time, then you're a lot smarter than me."

The evening continued in the same bantering vein and, too soon, dessert and coffee had been served and consumed and it was time to say their goodbyes.

Beth, Carly and Megan swapped phone numbers and email addresses with Grace, promising to be in touch early in the week. Sarah would come by the house on Monday. Grace and Jack were asked to join Will and Becky for dinner at a local restaurant on Tuesday. Mac got a promise out of Grace to join him for a ride on Wednesday. All the O'Malley women would be meet-

ing for lunch on Thursday and invited Grace along. She
was expected for dinner again the following Friday night
and on Saturday they were all off to a rodeo in the next
county. A friend of Luke's was bareback riding and they
were going along to support him.

"I'm exhausted just thinking about the week," Grace
confided as they drove away from the ranch.

Jack didn't say anything for the longest time, causing Grace to look across at him and ask, "What's up?"

"I'm sorry about Will. And Luke."

"Don't be. It's touching that they care about your
welfare."

"Sometimes they care *too* much."

Grace let it ride. Deep down she wished there was
someone in the world who cared half as much about her.

Chapter Fourteen

Unfortunately, the evening didn't end as well as it started.

Soon after inviting him up for coffee, Grace had Jack's shirt half-off and was reaching for his belt buckle when her cell phone rang.

She was tempted to ignore it, but something niggled, so she glanced at the screen. It was Sally. She held up a finger to Jack and answered.

"Grace?" the other woman practically screeched.

"Yes, it's me, Sally. What's wrong?"

"It's Aaron, my youngest. He's having an asthma attack and nothing's working! Please, please help me! I called 9-1-1, but they're in Silver Springs and you're much closer!"

Sally's panic was palpable. Grace needed to calm her down.

"I'll be there as soon as I can," she said, then put the phone to her chest and asked Jack, "Can you take me to Harper's Corner? Sally thinks her son is having an asthma attack."

She returned her attention to the mother. "Just stay on the line, Sally, if that makes you feel better."

Moments later, Jack had Betsy in gear, and they

peeled out of the parking lot and headed out of town toward the community of Harper's Corner. "I'm going to call the ambulance back on Jack's phone, Sally. If the asthma protocols aren't working, then it sounds like Aaron's had an allergic reaction to something and I need to make sure they have an EpiPen. As soon as I'm done with them, I'll be right back. We'll be there as soon as we can. In the meantime, elevate his legs and cover him with a blanket."

She called 9-1-1. After quickly explaining the situation to dispatch, she was put through to the ambulance, told them where she was going and checked that they had an EpiPen.

"Thank goodness you were there, Jack," she said as she waited for Sally to come back to her phone.

"Grace?"

"The ambulance is on it's way," she assured the panicked mother. "And we'll be there in…" She glanced across at Jack to get his input on how long it would take. "Two minutes," she reported as Jack held up two fingers. "Just hang in there, honey."

JACK GLANCED ACROSS at Grace as he heard her voice break on the last few words. Tears filled her eyes. "I'm so scared, Jack," she confessed. "This little boy could die!"

Jack pressed Betsy's accelerator to the floor, willing everything from his aged truck. He was already driving way over the speed limit, but it wouldn't hurt to get as much as Betsy could give.

She didn't handle so well on the turns as they sped toward Harper's Corner, but Grace didn't protest as—

in spite of wearing a seat belt—she was flung from one side of the bench seat to the other.

"What street?" Jack demanded as they neared the tiny settlement of Harper's Corner. It was in the opposite direction from Silver Springs and the hospital and ambulance center, so it was understandable that Sally had called Grace for help. The ambulance would be at least another five minutes away.

"Pine. Third house on the right. Her husband is waiting outside so we won't miss it."

Jack tore past the twenty-five-mile-an-hour sign as they arrived at Harper's Corner and quickly located Pine Street. Shifting Betsy down, her gears shrieking at the harsh treatment, Jack took the corner onto Pine too fast. But Betsy was up to it and recovered.

"There!" Grace said, spotting Sally's husband waving to them.

The man was whiter than a ghost as he opened Grace's door almost before the truck had come to a standstill. She leaped out and followed him inside the house.

"Good girl," Jack muttered, patting Betsy's dash and cutting the engine. He sat still for a few minutes, catching his breath. He'd thought Betsy might rattle apart on some of those corners, but she'd made it. She'd proven herself yet again.

Since the child's father had disappeared into the house with Grace, there was no one to meet the ambulance, so he flicked on Betsy's hazard lights, found his flashlight in the glove box and got out.

SALLY'S FACE WAS streaked with tears as she sat on the floor of the living room holding her child against her. Dex held his son's legs elevated as Grace had instructed.

Fortunately, Grace had managed to regain her composure by the time she knelt in front of Sally to check the boy's vitals.

Aaron was displaying all the outward symptoms of a severe asthma attack. Pale, sweaty face, blue lips, nostrils flaring and wheezing as he fought for his breath and then tried to exhale it. His pulse was rapid and he was almost unconscious.

"Nothing was working!" Sally wailed, and Grace knew she was talking about the bronchodilators prescribed for asthmatics. "Why wouldn't they work?"

Grace could only shake her head and say, "You did everything right, Sally. I think he's had an allergic reaction. Does he have any food allergies?"

Sally said no, and Grace gently turned the child over and lifted his pajama top, running her hands over his back, feeling for any bites. As she reached his shoulder, she felt something rough caught in the fabric. She grasped it and brought out a bee.

"I think we've found our culprit," Grace said, as she searched for the wound, found it and removed the stinger. Unless the ambulance arrived soon, Aaron's life was in grave danger.

Sally wrung her hands, saying, "I wish I'd never had that stupid dream of raising my kids outside the confines of town!"

"Don't go blaming yourself," Grace said, trying to keep the panic from her voice as she continued to monitor the child.

"Is he going to die?" Sally asked, her own voice almost a whisper.

"Not if I can help it," Grace said.

Then Aaron stopped breathing.

OUTSIDE, JACK COULD hear the wail of the ambulance. He ran to the end of the street, swinging his flashlight to attract their attention. Spotting him, the ambulance screamed through town and turned into Pine Street.

It pulled up behind Betsy, her hazard lights still flashing. Two paramedics leaped out and grabbed medical kits from the rear. The noise had woken several neighbors who now crowded around, curious.

"This way!" Jack shouted to the paramedics as he led them through the front gate. Grace was on her knees giving the boy mouth-to-mouth. The mother and father were clinging to each other, crying.

One of the paramedics knelt on the floor beside Grace and opened his kit.

"EpiPen?" Grace gasped between breaths. One of the paramedics handed it to her, she released the blue safety cap and plunged it into the child's thigh, watching for any change in Aaron's condition. Then she moved aside so the paramedics could fit an oxygen mask on his face.

Aaron moaned and his eyes flickered open.

"YOU LOOK EXHAUSTED," Jack said as he pulled up at Grace's apartment.

"I am." She rubbed her eyes and smiled across at him. "It's been quite a night."

"You were amazing."

"No more amazing than you and Betsy giving your all."

"And you're way too modest."

Grace shrugged. "Anyone with training could've saved Aaron," she said, wanting to downplay the situation.

"I'll take you upstairs." Jack cut the ignition and, with a hand under Grace's elbow, walked up the steps with her.

In their haste they'd both forgotten to lock the door—not that it mattered. Break-ins were rare in Spruce Lake.

"Home, sweet home," Grace muttered as she walked inside and turned to Jack, ready to thank him for all his help.

But he took her in his arms and kissed her, sending warmth through her body. She lifted her hands to rest on his shoulders, then slid them down his back, loving the feel of hard muscle beneath his shirt.

Jack kissed her long and hard, then drew back. "Good night, Grace," he said, releasing her abruptly. "Sleep tight." And before she could protest, he was gone.

Head spinning, confused by Jack's hasty departure, Grace staggered into her bedroom. Dog-tired, she tumbled onto the bed, scrunched a pillow beneath her head and was asleep within moments.

Chapter Fifteen

Grace didn't stir until nearly noon. Feeling half-doped, she flopped onto her back and stared at the ceiling, allowing the events of the previous night to play in her head.

She'd promised Sally she'd look in on Aaron today. A mother's love for and devotion to her child was a wondrous thing. Aaron couldn't have a better mom and she needed to tell Sally that. The poor woman blamed herself that Aaron's medications hadn't worked, but none of it was her fault.

Grace reached for her purse where she'd dropped it by the bed and drew out the photo of her daughter. Maybe it was time to write and ask for a more recent shot. Trying to guess what Amelia looked like now was tearing Grace apart. Maybe being so close to Jack had Grace thinking of her more often, wondering which of them she took after.

She might have come to Spruce Lake on an impulse, but now that she was here, she was determined to make up for not keeping in better touch with Aunt Missy while she was alive. She'd confided in Missy about her pregnancy and the old lady had been delighted that Grace had named her daughter Amelia, after her. And not once had she passed judgment on Grace's decision to give the baby away.

The house was now her daughter's legacy. Missy would enjoy the irony that it was Amelia's parents who were bringing it back to life together.

Shaking away her thoughts, Grace replaced the photo, then undressed and stepped into the shower.

After putting on denim shorts, a camisole top and a chambray shirt, with the buttons undone, she scooped her hair into a ponytail and set to work cleaning her tiny apartment.

It didn't take more than half an hour. She sat on her sofa and looked around. What to do now? The weekend stretched in front of her, long and lonely. She could always lie down and catch a few more z's, she supposed, but then she wouldn't sleep tonight. What she really needed was caffeine.

As if he had read her mind, she heard a knock, followed by Jack's voice calling through her door. "Wake up, sleepyhead, I've got coffee."

When Grace opened the door, her heart skipped a beat.

Jack stood there smiling, more masculine and desirable than ever. He held two take-out cups. She grinned and stood back to let him enter. "What's up?"

"Wanted to see how you were doing. And to invite you for a picnic."

"To check out the wildflowers on the mountains?" she asked, and took a sip of coffee, enjoying the caffeine rush. Spending time in nature was something she planned on doing a lot of here. So far she'd only managed to smell the flowers spilling out of the many planter boxes in town.

"I thought you might like to come to my cabin."

Now that was an invitation she couldn't refuse. "Sure! Let me get a blanket. I saw one stored in the closet."

"No need, I've got everything at my place."

"Can I bring anything else?"

"Nope, just you and your coffee."

"Sounds like a plan," Grace said, grabbing her purse and keys.

As Jack drove down Main Street, she called Sally.

"Oh, Grace! I don't know what we would have done without you last night," she said. "I'm sure we would have lost our little boy!"

"How is he this morning?" Grace asked.

"Aaron's fine. He's still in the hospital under observation, and while he's there, Dex and I are checking houses to rent in Silver Springs. We're determined to move as close to the hospital as possible. I couldn't go through last night again.

"Jack's given us a few rental leads. I'm starting to feel like we're a part of the community, and I really like that feeling."

"I'm glad to hear it, Sally. If you need anything, or have any concerns, just give me a call and I'll be right over."

"Thank you! I don't know what I'd do without you, Grace."

Embarrassed by the heartfelt praise, Grace said, "You concentrate on finding somewhere that'll suit your family, okay?"

"Sure. Have a great picnic with Jack!"

Grace had said her goodbyes before she realized that Sally already knew about Jack's agenda for the day.

"Everything all right?" he asked, turning at a fork in the road that Grace knew led to a valley farther from town than Two Elk.

"Fine. She told me to have a great picnic."

Jack grinned. "I have a confession. The picnic wasn't all my idea."

"Really?" Grace said with a chuckle.

"Sally called earlier today asking if I knew of any rental properties in Silver Springs, since she and Dex decided they need to live closer to the hospital. She suggested I take you on a picnic."

"So *none* of this was your idea?" Grace teased.

"The coffee was. And the location of the picnic."

Grace sat back and took in the scenery as the valley unfolded. "Fair enough," she said, and sipped her coffee. "You seem to have a lot of contacts around this area."

Jack tilted his head in acknowledgment. "Happens when you've lived somewhere pretty much all your life."

Grace pondered that remark. How different her upbringing had been from Jack's. He'd had the stability of a large, close-knit family and a beautiful home on a ranch, while her small family—if you could call it that—had drifted from one state to the next, never putting down roots for long. And although she'd spent the past dozen years living in Boston, it still didn't really feel like *home* to Grace.

She straightened, startled at the realization.

"What's up?" Jack asked.

She glanced across at him. He looked so comfortable, one arm draped casually over Betsy's steering wheel, the other resting on the window frame. The wind ruffled his hair, and he looked relaxed, at home. Safe.

Something clawed at Grace, deep inside. She felt the urge to curl up at Jack's side. Have him wrap an arm around her, draw her closer. Tell her he'd never let her go.

"Are you okay, sweetheart?"

Grace snapped out of her reverie. Had Jack just called her *sweetheart*? Was that an endearment she wanted to hear? Or not?

Jack turned off the road and onto a dirt track, then pulled over.

"Are we here?" Grace asked, looking at the pine forest around them.

"No. But you seem a bit spaced out. What's wrong?"

The concern in his voice touched her in the place where longing resided—the longing she tried so hard to repress.

No one was ever concerned about her. She was concerned about others, *cared* about others, cared *for* others! Grace's job, her life, wasn't a two-way street. She rarely took anything for herself. No time out, no life, no love. Yet here was Jack, causing those longings to surface and demand attention.

"Grace?"

She unfastened her seat belt and scooted across the seat to snuggle up to him. "Hold me. Just hold me, Jack," she said, unable to articulate anything more than that.

Silently, Jack complied, tucking her shoulder beneath his arm and wrapping the other protectively around her.

Grace closed her eyes and drew in a slow breath,

then let it out. For the first time in too many years, she felt truly at peace.

They sat like that for long minutes, Jack holding her, imparting his strength and his warmth. He stroked her hair. "What's up?" he finally asked again.

"Just feeling sorry for myself and in need of a hug."

"Want to talk about it?"

Grace eased out of Jack's embrace and looked up at him. She wouldn't burden him with her secrets, the things she'd kept to herself all her life. Particularly the secret involving him. "Not at the moment." She fixed her gaze on the windscreen. "Thanks for the offer, though."

Grace could feel his eyes on her before he started Betsy up and they continued along the dirt road. Eventually the forest thinned and they crossed a creek.

As Betsy heaved from side to side on the rough bridge over river stones, Grace said, "You sure like to take a girl to interesting places."

"Only special girls," Jack said quietly.

"How many special girls?" she asked, unable to stop herself.

"Just one."

Wistfully, she asked, "What was her name?"

"Grace."

"You mean me?"

"I don't see any other Grace, do you?"

"I...thought you would've brought a lot of girls out here."

"Why would you think that?"

Flustered, she said, "Oh, for heaven's sake, Jack, you're the most eligible bachelor in Spruce Lake!"

"Excuse me?"

Grace's attention was diverted by the small cabin that came into view. "Is this your house?" she asked, sitting forward. "It's adorable!"

DISTRACTED, JACK COULD only smile. Confronted by his simple abode, a renovated miner's shack, Grace seemed enchanted.

"I don't know that it qualifies as a house, but yes, it's what I call home. One of these days, I'm going to build something more substantial on this lot, but for now, it works for me."

"One of these days?" Grace said. "One of these days when you marry and have children?"

He cut the engine and looked across at her. "That's the plan, yes."

Her light brown eyes clouded and she turned away. "Whoever marries you, Jack, will be a very lucky woman."

The comment sliced right through Jack's heart. Grace didn't think she'd be that woman.

Resolved that somehow, some way, he would change her mind, Jack helped her out the driver's side.

"It was a burned-out shell when I got it. I had some of the guys labor on this whenever we had a break between contracts. It was quite an eye-opener for them to work on such a wreck, especially since one of them had been arrested for arson."

"Did he spend time in jail for it?"

"No, Kyle was only fourteen at the time, but he went to juvie. A contact back in L.A. recommended him to me when he got out. It was a good project for him to understand the damage caused by arson, even though no one was living here at the time." He opened the door and let Grace in ahead of him. "No one worked harder on this project than that kid. It was as if he needed to atone for his sins. He slept under the stars and worked from dawn till late every day. He learned a lot about carpentry—and himself."

Grace wondered if she could ever atone for her own sins. There were so many. How she'd even start to make amends for keeping her secret from Jack, she had no idea.

"Where is he now?"

"He's an apprentice plumber with one of the contractors I use. You might meet him at Adam's house tomorrow."

At her frown, he explained. "In spite of Adam's assurances that Carly wants to stay in town, I'd like to get their place at least weather-tight before winter. I was hoping you'd like to come along. Kyle and a couple of the guys will be there. For some strange reason they enjoy spending some of their weekends with my family."

Grace laughed at that. "Who *wouldn't* want to spend time with your family? They're wonderful. And so is this," Grace said, indicating the cabin. "You're not going to demolish it when you build the bigger house, are you?"

"Nope. I'll keep it for guests. Maybe emergency housing for kids in need." He shrugged. "I haven't thought that far ahead. Not much point, since I can't find anyone to marry me."

Jack lifted a hand to her cheek. "Actually, I *have* found her. Unfortunately, she doesn't want to marry me."

"What do you want from me, Jack?"

"I want you to marry me."

"That's a very strange way to ask."

"Would it help if I got down on one knee?"

"No."

"Didn't think so."

"Can we make a pact to forget about talk of marriage and just enjoy ourselves today?"

"Okay. But I want you to know it's never far from my thoughts."

"Jack, I'm sorry, but I didn't come back to Spruce Lake to get into a relationship. I left Boston to get away from one."

"And you succeeded. Come and live here. Marry me."

Grace walked farther into the cabin, then turned to him. "I wish I hadn't messed everything up, Jack. I was so ambitious, so desperate to get away from my parents and the unhappy memories of my childhood. I needed to show them I was better than them, that I would never want for money or respect." She gestured helplessly and Jack's heart went out to her. "If I could take it all back, start my life over, I'd do things so differently."

Moved—and a little puzzled—by her revelation, he opened the fridge and pulled out sandwich fixings.

"I don't feel hungry now, if you don't mind, Jack."

He faltered. Maybe he was part of the bad memories she wanted to escape.

"Should I take you back to town?"

"No, I want to be with you, but please, can we not talk about us?"

"Okay," he said, relieved, and desperate not to upset her further. "How about if we make these sandwiches and take them on a hike? The view from the mountain is spectacular. You'll have an appetite by the time we climb up there."

"I could be dead by the time we climb up there! Remember, I was at sea level less than a week ago. I haven't adapted to the altitude yet."

"Then I'll piggyback you to the top."

Grace laughed and Jack reveled in the sound of it. "Watch out! I may take you up on it."

Jack shrugged and smiled. "I have strong shoulders."

He noticed the way Grace's eyes shifted from his face to his shoulders, and turned back to the fridge to hide his reaction to her.

"Are you making the sandwiches *in* the fridge? You've had your head buried in there long enough."

He grabbed mustard and mayo and closed the door with his foot. You'd think at thirty he'd be able to control his baser urges, but no, whenever Grace was near, he was aroused!

He sliced the multigrain loaf, then piled the slices to the side of the cutting board.

"I can help," Grace said, brushing against him and picking up a knife. "Mayo, mustard or both?"

"Both," he said, not thinking. They needed to leave the confines of the cabin. Maybe this wasn't such a good idea, bringing Grace here. It was too isolated, too intimate.

Jack wasn't convinced that Grace simply wanted to

avoid another relationship. There was more to it than that, he was sure.

If he was going to get her to marry him, he needed to take it slow, let her fall in love with him again.

Chapter Sixteen

So many people had dropped by the house on Monday morning—including Sarah—that Grace was wondering if she'd ever get a chance to relax.

Exhausted after the picnic hike with Jack, the Saturday evening concert and Sunday with the O'Malleys at Adam and Carly's house, Grace wanted nothing more than to pull up a deck chair and have a snooze on the porch.

The latest visitor was someone she'd never met before, although she knew the woman's brother.

Grace had stopped sweeping up yet another pile of sawdust and plaster when she heard the front gate squeak.

A tall, fair-haired woman strode up the path and mounted the few steps to the porch. She held out her hand and said, "Hi, Grace, I'm Lucy Cochrane, Mike's sister and an old school friend of Matt's." Mike Cochrane was the lawyer who'd sweet-talked Jack into taking on this project.

Grace dusted her palms on her jeans and shook Lucy's hand. "I've heard of you. You're the local OB/GYN?"

"That's right. And that's what I've come to talk to you about."

Grace frowned slightly. She didn't need an OB/GYN. She crossed her arms and leaned against the railing. "I have a gynecologist back in Boston and I'm not pregnant, so I don't really need another."

Lucy laughed and leaned against the railing, too. Grace noted her height—she easily topped six feet. "No, I came to offer you a business proposition."

"Oh?" Grace had never had one before and she wasn't sure how to proceed. "I'm a pediatrician, not a business-woman," she said.

Lucy's eyes twinkled. "You're a woman who owns a large house on prime real estate."

"Sorry, the house isn't for sale."

Smiling, Lucy said, "I didn't expect it to be. Can I take you to lunch at Maria's and outline what I have in mind?"

Intrigued, Grace could only accept the invitation. "Okay," she said. "Just let me wash up and let the boss know I'm leaving for an early lunch. Would you like to come in?" she asked, leading the way to the front door.

They stepped inside and Lucy gasped. "Wow! I always wondered what this place looked like. It's even better than I imagined."

Grace glanced around, mystified. "They've ripped out the kitchen and the interior walls in order to insulate them, and torn up a lot of the flooring. Trust me, it looked a whole lot nicer last week, even though it hadn't been lived in for years."

Lucy grinned and said, "No, I meant the space!" She indicated the two-level foyer, the wide staircase and the size of the downstairs rooms.

"Do you mind if I take a look upstairs?" Lucy asked.

"Be my guest," Grace said. "I'll wash up and meet you back down here."

She watched as Lucy dashed up the stairs. The woman had an athletic body and a fluid grace. She could've been a professional athlete, Grace decided as she entered the downstairs bathroom and washed her hands.

It was a good few minutes before Lucy joined her again.

"It's perfect!" she said as she came downstairs and into the foyer.

Lucy had obviously been impressed with the capacious rooms upstairs, as well.

"Ready?" Grace asked.

"Sure. Want to walk? Nothing's far from this place."

Grace nodded. As they left the house, she said, "It's one of the reasons I decided to get rid of my rental car. I figure I can walk anywhere I need to from here."

She spotted Tyrone coming around the side of the house and said, "Tyrone, would you mind telling Mr. O'Malley I've taken an early lunch? I looked for him but Buzz said he's gone out."

Tyrone's smile lit up his face. "Sure, Ms. Grace. See you later." He rubbed a hand along the railings she'd been sanding. "Boss won't like the job you've been doin' here. I'll fix it before he finds out, okay?"

Grace laughed. "You know his exacting standards too well! Thanks, Tyrone, I owe you."

Tyrone gave her a little salute, and set to work on the railings.

"Nice kid," Lucy said as Grace held open the gate. "Jack does wonders with all the kids who come here.

I have to admit, Tyrone scared me when I first met him—a kid with too much attitude and a bad reputation. But Jack seems to see through all that. He gives the kids respect, somewhere safe to live and an honest day's work. It doesn't take him long to turn them around."

The two women spent the short walk to Maria's diner discussing Jack's program for disadvantaged youths. Lucy obviously admired Jack for what he was achieving with the kids. It made Grace glow with prided.

At Maria's, Lucy picked a table that looked out on the street, but was farthest from other patrons and any potential interruption.

Almost before they'd sat down, Maria was at their table, pouring glasses of water. "Dr. Lucy, Dr. Grace! How nice to see you. Can I get you something else to drink?"

Lucy looked up and smiled at Maria. "How are your children, Maria?" To Grace, she said, "I delivered all three of them. Each one an angel!"

"Hah!" Maria scoffed. "I don't have enough hours in the day to complain about what rascals those boys of mine are. They all take after their father!"

The three women laughed, then Lucy said, "I'll have the usual, Maria. Chocolate milk shake and your delicious wilted spinach salad with goat cheese."

Grace hadn't had a milk shake since she was a teenager and it sounded appealing. So did the salad. "I'll have the same," she said, handing her menu back to Maria.

She crossed her arms and rested them on the table. "So, what's this about a business proposition?"

"Well," Lucy said, mirroring her action, "I need

space for my practice. So do some other professionals in town, and I've been thinking your house is the perfect location for a clinic that offers family medicine, medical specialties, physical therapy and so on."

Grace was dumbfounded. Finally, she found her voice. "*My* house? You want to convert my house into a medical center?"

Lucy nodded. "That's the idea." Taking advantage of Grace's lack of response, she plowed on. "I live in town, but my practice is in Silver Springs. And I'm paying a fortune for the space! My patients will follow me if I relocate. And it would be a whole lot more convenient to be closer to my kids and their school."

"But…you deliver babies at the hospital," Grace pointed out.

"True, but we all know babies don't arrive as quickly as they do in movies. And if they come quickly, like in under thirty minutes, I've never actually made it to the hospital to deliver them, anyway!"

Grace laughed at that. "Granted, but why my house? Why not anywhere in Spruce Lake? There's parking to consider, as well."

Lucy held up her fingers and counted off the reasons. "It's the perfect size—large reception area downstairs and treatment rooms upstairs. It's in a great location, just off Main Street but an easy walk to everything. It's got historical charm that screams Spruce Lake— rather than a purpose-built brick box in another area. I think patients and clients will feel more comfortable somewhere homey. Parking? There's a big backyard. We could even make the house wheelchair accessible with a ramp out back. Plus, there's a wide laneway out back and a vacant lot that no one wants to build on because it's cut off from everything else. We could buy it and turn it into the patients' parking lot."

"We?" Grace squeaked. "All my spare cash is tied up in that house and the renovation."

Undaunted, Lucy said, "I'm positive we could sort something out. The street in front of the house is extra-wide, so maybe the town would be amenable to angle parking—"

Grace made the time-out sign, thankful that it halted Lucy's speech. "There's an awful lot of ifs, buts and maybes involved in this. That's a historically listed house. I'm not actually sure it *could* be converted into a medical center."

"But are you amenable to my ideas?"

"Amenable! I don't know if your ideas are even sane," Grace said, then softened her words with a smile.

Lucy laughed and said, "I can't blame you for thinking I'm a bit crazy. Jack said you were going to renovate the house but didn't intend to live in it."

"I can't see myself staying here, especially all alone in that big house," Grace said.

"Wouldn't you live there with Jack?"

"Now, why would I live there with Jack?"

"Because he's the most eligible bachelor in town—if not the entire state of Colorado. And he's in love with you."

Grace could feel her face heating. "And you know this because…?"

"The whole town knows! No one around here can keep a secret and when word spread that Jack's old girlfriend was back—the one who broke his heart and…" Lucy's words trailed off.

"Gee, thanks. Next they'll be blaming me for global warming."

Maria arrived with their salads and milk shakes. "Thanks, Maria," Lucy said. "Looks delicious, as usual." Once Maria was gone, she launched back into the conversation.

"Global warming? Hadn't thought of that one, maybe you did cause it?" She winked and picked up her fork.

"I think I've lost my appetite," Grace said, staring at the plate piled with spinach, caramelized walnuts, goat cheese and other goodies.

"You don't like the salad?"

"No, it's fine. I don't like the thought of everyone talking about Jack and me. Poking their noses into our business."

"So you *are* an item!" Lucy said, apparently latching on to the words *our business*.

"No, we're not." Grace dug into her lunch. She finished the mouthful and said, "You're right. This is a great choice." Sipping the milk shake she closed her eyes in bliss. "This, too. Now, can we drop any reference to Jack and me and get on with your insane idea for my house?"

"Will you consider it?"

The idea was so new to Grace, so unformed, that she hadn't had time to process it. But since she had to keep the house in the family, maybe repurposing it wasn't such a bad suggestion. "I think we need to do a whole lot more research. For instance, it could take years to find tenants for all the treatment rooms. *If* the council even lets us turn it into a clinic."

Lucy swallowed some of her milk shake and said, "Not so. There's me, you, Harley James the physical therapist, Suze Wilson the counselor and Carly O'Malley the massage therapist."

Apart from Carly O'Malley, the others' names blurred together as Grace focused on one word—*you.*

"Hold it! What do you mean *you?* As in *me?*"

"Yes, of course, I mean you! I know you're a pediatrician, but this town needs a really good family practitioner and you'd be great in that role."

"What about Doc Jenkins?"

"He's retiring at the end of the week. Thank goodness! Should've been put out to pasture long ago." As if sensing Grace's hesitation, she pushed her plate away and rested her forearms on the table. "This is a growing town, Grace. You could make a good living here. I heard what you did for Sally's son Aaron. If you weren't there, he might not have made it. We need good doctors. If we set up this clinic, we will attract *more* good doctors. We have orthopedic guys who visit during the winter, but they work out of the emergency center. And they need somewhere to refer patients for physical therapy. Harley wants to move his practice here. Susan needs space for her clients. Same with Carly."

Grace shook her head. "I can't believe you've rounded up all these people so fast."

Lucy smiled. "It's not as shocking as it sounds. We've been discussing for months that we wanted a clinic in Spruce Lake, but there's nowhere big enough for all of us to rent. But your house is. Picture this, Grace." Lucy gestured in the air. "Patients and clients come into the foyer to a front desk. They have a lovely, big, light-filled waiting room—where the present living room is. The dining room can be converted into office space for the staff. The drawing room could easily be converted into a couple of consulting rooms and then upstairs are more exam and treatment rooms, as well as bathrooms. We can all share in the front counter staff, thereby cutting costs. Can you imagine people gathered on the front porch during the summer, enjoying the fresh air, relaxing before their appointments? The older patients waiting in a safe environment to be collected by loved ones or the staff from the Twilight Years? That big eat-in kitchen would be ideal as a lunch room and even for staff meetings. It's a no-brainer, Grace!"

Grace held up her hands. "Stop!"

Lucy halted and Grace said, "I can't believe I'm saying this, but it's all starting to sound like it could work."

"Yay!" Lucy cried, causing several customers to glance in her direction.

"Not so fast," Grace said. "First, we need to secure parking. And find out if we can get permits to run a medical center there—and even if we're allowed to convert the house into something other than a residential building, then we need to talk to Jack."

"I don't see that as a problem."

"What? The permits—or Jack?"

"Either. The town wants a medical center that caters to a range of issues. And a renovation is a renovation to Jack. Doesn't matter if it's a house into a house or a house into a medical center."

"How can you be so sure?"

Lucy had the grace to flush. "Uh, I saw him last night and ran the idea by him."

"I see." Grace felt strangely betrayed that Jack hadn't mentioned it this morning. Still, Lucy's idea was growing on her. "How soon do you think we can talk to the town about this?"

As Lucy nearly leaped over her seat to hug her, Grace waved her back down. "Just so you understand, agreeing to talk to the town doesn't mean I've agreed to this, okay?"

"You will," Lucy said, looking far too pleased. She slurped the last of her milk shake. "Harley and Suze would love to meet you. Carly, of course, you already know. And once word gets out, I don't see any problems filling the other rooms."

Grace liked Lucy and liked her energy and enthusiasm. With friends like her, Sally and the O'Malley women, she could almost see herself settling in Spruce Lake. And perhaps even being happy here.

HAVING LEFT LUCY with the task of arranging meetings with the relevant authorities, Grace walked through the front gate and up the porch steps, deep in thought. So deep, in fact, that she slammed smack into Will O'Malley as he came out the door. He grabbed her arms before she fell backward.

"Whoa there!" he said. "Where have you been all day? I hear Tyrone's fingers are sanded to the bone."

Grace laughed and offered her cheek for a kiss. Lily was in a toddler carrier strapped to his back. She held out her hand and Grace smooched it, making noises that had the toddler giggling. Then she felt a wet tongue on her leg and looked down. A dog that was mostly black Labrador gazed adoringly up at her, then wagged her tail and rubbed her face against Grace's leg.

"Hello," Grace said, kneeling to pet her. "What's your name, girl?" The dog tried to lick her face and Grace leaned back. She loved dogs but wasn't fond of doggie kisses.

"How'd you know Millie was a girl?" Will asked.

"The pink scarf around her neck? The fact that she has teats, meaning she's nursing or has recently weaned a litter?" Grace said as she stood. Millie continued to lean against her.

"She your dog?" Grace asked.

"Nope, she's yours," Will said, handing the leash to her.

"Mine?" Grace knew Will was a little eccentric, so she played along.

"Millie's puppies have all been adopted from the animal shelter and she needs a loving home now."

"And naturally your first sucker was me?"

"Yup. First and only."

"That's pretty presumptuous of you."

Will held up a hand as if taking the oath. "Guilty as charged."

"She has three legs."

"You noticed that, too?"

Will was incorrigible. Grace couldn't help smiling. "What I mean is, if she has three legs, then someone must've loved her enough to pay for the surgery."

Will shook his head. "She was found beside the highway—we think she was dumped because she was pregnant. And she probably got hit by a car because her front leg was so badly mangled it had to be removed."

"We?"

"The animal shelter and me."

"You found her?"

"Yup. Since Becky wasn't partial to having another dog in the house—we've already got two—I took her to the shelter, paid for the operation and promised to find homes for her and the pups."

Grace shook her head. Will really did have a heart of gold. Tears burned her eyes at the thought that others could be so unkind to animals. To hide them, she knelt so her face was at Millie's level. This time, she allowed the dog to lick her. Then, feeling overwhelmed with emotion, she hugged the dog to her, burying her face in the soft black fur. Millie whimpered and leaned even closer to Grace.

"I'm not sure Mrs. C. would let me keep her in the apartment," Grace said into Millie's coat, hiding the catch in her voice. And trying for one last feeble excuse not to complicate her life by allowing an animal into it.

"Not a problem! In fact, she's offered to take Millie for walks if you can't get home at lunchtime."

Grace stood and looked into Will's eyes. They were completely guileless. "You have it all figured out, don't you? Ever since I came into town, you had me earmarked for Millie."

Will shrugged. "What can I say? You're perfectly matched."

"I'm not missing a leg."

"True. But you both need someone to love."

Grace could feel the tears again. They spilled out and ran down her cheeks.

"Come here," Will said, dragging her into his arms and against his broad chest. "You're not alone anymore, Grace. You have Millie and all of us O'Malleys and anyone who's met you in this town."

Grace half laughed, half sobbed as she asked, "Even Loosie Lettie and Jamie the Jerk?"

He rubbed her back. "Only if you want them. Although I have to say, they *are* two people who aren't exactly singing your prais—"

"Hey!"

Jack's shout had them jumping apart. He marched up to Will and said, "Get your hands off my girlfriend."

His possessiveness both thrilled and alarmed Grace and then she saw that he was joking.

"Your *girlfriend* was just thanking me for Millie." Will indicated the dog who hadn't moved from Grace's feet.

"Stop talking about me as if I'm not here!" she protested.

Jack bent down to ruffle Millie's ears. "So you've agreed to adopt her, have you?"

"I have," she said, and looked up at Will. "One thing, has she been spayed?"

"She's booked for next week. Bit cruel to have her in stitches while she was still nursing."

"Agreed. So you'll let me know when and where?"

Will beamed and Grace suspected he hadn't been one hundred percent sure until just then that Millie had found a home.

She glanced at Jack. "What a shame I can't stay and

sand the railings some more. I have to go to the super-market and get food and a bowl and a dog bed for Mil-lie. Bye," she said, twinkling her fingers at the two men and heading down the stairs, Millie at her heels. It was as though the dog *knew* she belonged to Grace now.

"Here, catch!" Jack called, and tossed Betsy's keys to Grace. She caught them neatly, then bent to grab Mil-lie's leash as it trailed along the path. "Thanks," she said. "You can pick Betsy up at my place later. I'll be too busy with Millie to come here again today."

She saw Jack grin as she turned away. Feeling hap-pier than she had in a long time, Grace practically skipped down the street to Betsy. She opened the pas-senger door and gave Millie a boost in. Millie gazed longingly out the window at Grace, who climbed in and ruffled the dog's furry neck. "You and I are going to be a great pair, Millie," she said.

Millie rewarded her by licking her hand, then peered out the windshield as if looking forward to a new ad-venture with her new mistress.

GRACE ARRIVED HOME with a bit more than she'd intended to buy. When she'd set off from Aunt Missy's, she fig-ured she'd be able to carry home a bag of kibble, a dog bed and a bowl from the supermarket. It was just as well that Jack had lent her his truck, she thought as she lifted Millie out, then reached in for the goodies she'd pur-chased. Millie waited patiently while Grace unloaded the bags, then turned toward the stairs leading up to the apartment. Millie hopped up the steps beside her, clearly determined not to be left behind.

When Grace let herself and Millie into the apartment, she looked down at the dog, who stood uncertainly on the threshold. "This is your home now, Millie. Come on!"

Wagging her tail, Millie raced inside and inspected her new lodgings, sniffing the furniture as Grace wrestled the bags into the living room and dumped them on the floor. Millie sat at her feet and studied Grace expectantly. Grace patted the sofa beside her and Millie jumped up, settled herself with her nose resting on Grace's leg and watched as she unpacked the bags.

"Here's your water bowl," Grace said, showing the shiny bowl to Millie. Millie sniffed it and wagged her tail. "And here's your food bowl." The action was repeated by Millie, who was then plied with all manner of chew toys, throw toys, squeaking toys, snuggle toys and a supply of poop bags.

Finally, Grace pulled out a collar. On it, she fastened a diamante-encrusted tag displaying Millie's name and Grace's cell number, along with a charm depicting Saint Francis—patron saint of animals. Grace then buckled the collar around Millie's neck, leaving the pink scarf in place, as well.

"There! Now you're all set to go out into the world!" Grace said. "Shall we go play ball in the park?"

The words *park* and *ball* obviously resonated with Millie, who jumped off the sofa and trotted to the door.

"Just a minute, Millie. I need to take care of these groceries and then I'll be with you." In the kitchen, Grace put the fillet steaks, which she'd bought to grill on her balcony, in the fridge, as well as salad fixings and some beer. She hadn't yet asked Jack if he wanted to join her for dinner, but that wasn't a problem. If he couldn't make it, then Millie could have his share of the steak!

"So what do you think of converting the house to a medical center?" Grace asked as she prepared a salad to go with the steaks Jack was grilling.

"A renovation is a renovation. Might cost you a few pennies more, though," Jack said, leaning on the door frame leading to the balcony. The sun was setting behind him, the sky's colors glowing around him like an aura. The only jarring note was the pair of tongs he held, ready to turn the steaks.

Before grilling them, Grace had cut her steak in half to share with Millie, much to Jack's amusement. "Bet she didn't get fillet in the pound," he said as Grace cut the steak into smaller pieces and put it in Millie's bowl. The dog, of course, pounced on the treat and practically inhaled it. Then she looked around for more.

"Sorry. One steak per night," Grace told her, filling her bowl with a measured amount of kibble.

"You're a natural with her," Jack said. "Yet I don't recall you ever saying you had a dog growing up."

"I didn't." Grace stood and washed her hands at the sink. "But I always wanted one."

"You and your ex didn't have any pets?"

Grace made a face and said, "Please, can we not spoil a beautiful evening?"

"I'm just trying to find out more about you."

Which was exactly what Grace *didn't* want. "There's nothing to tell. Nothing worthwhile, anyway. So let's change the subject." Salad ready, she grabbed a glass of iced tea and joined Jack on the balcony. The smell of grilling steak filled the air. "I'm starving!" she said, and flopped into a deck chair. "Manual labor gives me an appetite."

"In which case, Tyrone should be eating up a storm tonight," Jack said, and laughed.

"You heard about that, did you?"

"Apart from the fact that I saw him working on the railings, I would've been able to tell from the finish that you sure hadn't done them," he teased.

"Oh, you think you're so smart!" Grace said, punching his arm lightly. "I'm officially quitting as a laborer on that project and taking on other duties instead."

"Which are?"

"Lucy's got us an appointment at the mayor's office in the morning. If we get the go-ahead, then I'll be tied up preparing permits and everything, so I won't have time to sand railings. Okay?"

She finished the last sentence on a challenging note, daring Jack to disagree.

He held up his hands. "Fine by me. You were taking too long to learn, anyway. And I didn't want your pretty little fingers near the electric saws."

"I'm getting a manicure in the morning and I'm *never* touching another tool. Deal?"

Jack beamed at her. "Deal."

They ate their salads outside, watching the last of the rays disappear behind the mountains. The evening started to chill quickly once the sunlight was gone. Grace got herself a sweater. She offered Jack a blanket but he shook his head and checked the steaks. "I think they're done," he said, and lifted them onto a plate to take inside.

Millie was curled up on her new bed, fast asleep. But when she got a whiff of the meat, her head rose and she looked around.

"Go back to sleep, sweetie," Grace said. "These are for the humans."

The dog stared as if waiting for her to change her mind. Realizing Grace wasn't going to, she put her head down on top of a cuddle toy she particularly liked—a bright yellow chicken covered in a soft furlike material. It surprised Grace, because it looked so unlike a puppy. But Millie seemed to like it, as she settled her nose over the chicken and went back to sleep.

JACK PLACED THE FILLETS on their plates, along with a baked potato each, then they sat at the small kitchen table to eat.

"These steaks are incredibly tender," Grace noted.

"Probably came from Two Elk," Jack said. "You don't have to buy them at the supermarket, you know. Pop will give you as much as you want."

"I'm sure he would, but I prefer to do it this way. I don't like taking charity."

"It wouldn't be charity. You're almost one of the family," Jack said, then seeing Grace's look of alarm, he shut up.

He couldn't believe how hard it was to coax Grace to open up about herself, what her life in Boston had been like, the experiences she'd had. He cast around for something else to talk about. Since Grace seemed enthusiastic about the medical center, he stuck to that topic.

But he intended to get the truth out of Grace. He just wasn't sure how to go about it yet.

Chapter Seventeen

Grace took care in dressing for her appointment with the mayor the following morning.

Having never met the eccentric Frank Farquar, she wasn't sure exactly how to present herself, but in the end decided on a navy shirtdress and sensible flat pumps. Satisfied she looked businesslike—without risking her Christian Louboutin heels on the cracked sidewalks— she said goodbye to Millie and popped into Mrs. C.'s to let her know she'd be out for a few hours, then headed in the direction of town hall.

Lucy was already there, waiting nervously with Beth O'Malley.

"Hey, Grace!" Lucy greeted her. "I hope you don't mind, but I invited Beth along. Since she's an architect, I thought she could give us a few pointers on redesigning the interior, and the mayor is kind of sweet on her, so every bit helps!"

"Of course I don't mind Beth being here, too," Grace assured her, and turned to Beth. "Thanks for joining us."

Grace didn't know Matt's wife very well. Beth exuded a cool confidence. She was tall, blond, blue-eyed and soft-spoken, but Grace detected a sharp intelligence beneath her serene exterior.

"I'm delighted to have been asked, Grace." She glanced at her watch. "Shall we go in? It's almost nine."

Grace noticed that Beth had a folder under her arm—the type that held large documents. She was curious about what was inside.

They were shown into a large room lined with cherrywood. At the end was a long table where three men sat. They rose from their chairs when introduced. The mayor was flanked by the town manager and the town planner. They didn't seem as intimidating as Grace had expected. As the meeting progressed, and especially when Beth produced three sets of blueprints of the new clinic and handed one to each man, they seemed very receptive to the idea.

Grace was more than a little surprised to see the plans labeled Saunders Medical Center. She was about to protest, when she saw the notation beneath—"Opened in loving memory of Amelia (Missy) Saunders, 1916–2006."

The mayor then waxed lyrical about his experiences as a boy growing up and his memories of Missy. Grace found them fascinating, an insight into a beloved great-aunt she really knew little about. The town planner and manager, however, looked bored.

Grace decided she needed to move things along so suggested, "Mayor Farquar, this is so interesting to me. Could I take you to lunch today so I can find out more about my aunt Missy?"

After the mayor had accepted her invitation, the planner spent some time explaining the types of permits they needed to apply for, while the manager took a closer look at the blueprints and made some notes. All in all,

Grace felt the meeting was going well, particularly when the manager said that the vacant lot behind the house was owned by the town and they'd be willing to lease it for parking. Furthermore, the planner added that he didn't see any reason the sidewalk couldn't be torn up, since it was in such a degraded condition—and a new sidewalk and an angle parking area could be created in front of the house!

An hour later, the three women stumbled out into the bright sunlight, bubbling with excitement. They high-fived one another. "You were fantastic!" Grace told Beth. "When did you draw up those floor plans?"

"Last night. I stopped by the house, took some measurements and spent a few hours working on them. With architectural software it's easy."

"But still, they're so detailed. I think the manager had blueprint envy."

Beth laughed. "I simply thought it would help our case if they had something concrete to look at."

"Which it did," Lucy pointed out. "However, there are a lot more hoops to jump through than I realized. This could take longer than expected, filling and filing all those forms."

"I quit as a laborer, so I have time on my hands," Grace said. "I'm good at dotting *i*'s and crossing *t*'s. And besides, if it's going to be my project, I should be doing the paperwork."

"Great!" Lucy and Beth said at once.

"I'm more than happy to give all of that to you, Grace," Lucy said, and checked her watch. "But I have to head over to Silver Springs right now. My clinic starts at the hospital in half an hour." She kissed Grace and Beth goodbye.

"I'm really impressed with those plans," Grace told Beth. "Do you mind if I have a copy to go over when it's not so hectic?"

"Of course." Beth opened the folder and drew out a set of blueprints for Grace. "Now, I have to run. The sheriff is minding our little cherub this morning," she said. "Matt was catching up on paperwork this morning, anyway, so he said he'd watch her while I came to the meeting." She placed a hand on Grace's arm. "I wish I could join you and the mayor for lunch. Can you and I reschedule for another day?"

"Of course!" Grace smiled. "But I'm running late, too—for a manicure," she said, showing her nails to Beth.

"Ugh!" Beth said. "Just as well you quit working on the house. Otherwise, you'd have no nails left."

"Agreed. And I much prefer paperwork. I have to confess I'm kind of glad Lucy came up with this idea. I'm so excited about it. I may even stay in Spruce Lake…."

"I was hoping you'd say that!" Beth said. "Does Jack know?"

Grace realized she'd revealed too much, particularly to someone who was close to Jack. "I'm sorry," she said. "Would you mind keeping that to yourself? I'm at a bit of a crossroads in my life, not sure where I want to live, where I want to practice…. I hate feeling like this, but I can't seem to shake it." Not only that, Grace had been receiving insistent emails from the clinic in Boston.

She couldn't make a decision about moving to Spruce Lake for good without considering all the ramifications.

"I'm no counselor," Beth said. "But I'm a good listener. If you want to talk about it, call me, okay?" She stopped beside her car. "Can I give you a ride? Are you going to Patty's?"

"I am," Grace confirmed.

"Then hop in and I'll have you there in no time!"

GRACE WAVED TO BETH as she drove off toward the sheriff's department. Nice person, she thought as she turned into Patty's Parlor.

Grace was so happy with her manicure—that Patty could resurrect her nails was truly miraculous in Grace's eyes—she stayed for a pedicure, as well. Feeling like a new woman, she walked the couple of blocks to Rusty's and pushed her way through the front door.

Mayor Farquar was already there, sitting in a booth so he wouldn't miss her as she walked inside. He looked ready for action, too. His napkin was tucked into his collar and he was drinking a beer.

"Now, little lady, what can I order you to drink?" he asked, standing until Grace settled herself in the opposite seat and calling over a waiter.

"A lemonade," she told him, and then turned her gaze on Mayor Farquar. She'd heard of him, of course, when she was a teenager, but at that time Frank had lived outside town at the quarry he owned. An eccentric bachelor. Since Grace had left, Frank had acquired a pet pig and a wife. In that order. Rumor had it he was fonder of his pig than his wife. Grace, having met Mrs. C., didn't believe a word of it.

"The wife tells me she's walking your dog today," he said.

Grace brightened. "Yes, she is. Mrs. Carmi—er, Farquar was so kind to offer."

"'S'okay, you can call her Mrs. C. I'm a modern man. I can understand she was a Carmichael longer than she's been a Farquar."

This was eye-opening news for Grace. She'd categorized the mayor as a bit of a good ol' boy who probably thought women belonged in the home and should obey their husbands without question.

"So," she said, leaning her forearms on the table, "tell me all you know about my great-aunt Missy. I was a selfish teen when we lived with her and never really recognized her significance to this town until recently."

The waiter returned and they ordered—a double bacon burger with a side of fries and another of onion rings for him, a grilled chicken Caesar salad for her. She should probably have a little chat with Frank about his diet, but now wasn't the time. Perhaps when they were better friends, she'd ask him to make an appointment to see her at the new clinic. The realization that she was making plans for her future shocked Grace a little.

"Missy was born right there in that house of yours, way back in 1916," Frank said, breaking into her thoughts.

"I'd heard that," Grace said. "But I don't have any photographs of her growing up there. I asked her about it once and she said they were all burned."

"That's a darned shame," Mayor Farquar said, "because they'd make a wonderful contribution to the town's archives. We now have a heritage museum on

Main Street in the old Methodist church Jack and his brother Will own. They let us use it rent-free."

"Not only am I clueless about my great-aunt Missy, but I don't know much about the properties Jack owns, either," Grace said.

"You gonna marry that boy?"

Stunned by his candor, Grace took a moment to answer. "No."

He shook his head. "That boy needs a wife. Someone who's his equal. Unless you don't think he's *your* equal, you bein' a big-city doctor an' all."

"No, of course I don't feel I'm better than Jack! Whatever gave you that idea?" Grace leaned back to make room for their plates. She felt sick looking at Frank's, piled with grease.

"Mayor Farquar—"

"Call me Frank, honey," he said, picking up his fork and digging into his fries.

"Frank, then. I need to be frank with you, Frank."

The older man looked up at her and grinned. "If I had a dollar for every time someone's said that, and then not been so frank, I'd be a millionaire."

From what Grace had heard, Frank Farquar *was* a millionaire. Several times over, thanks to rocks.

"Okay, then I'll be more than frank, Frank," she said with a smile to lessen what she had to say next. "As a doctor, I'm going to be brutally honest. You are a heart attack waiting to happen. You're overweight, you're wheezing just sitting down and now you're stuffing your face with pure grease."

Frank halted, the fatty burger halfway to his mouth, and put it back on his plate. His eyes narrowed. Maybe she'd overstepped her bounds. Grace had dealt with overweight children, but they were overweight because the parents couldn't say no to their little darlings and let them eat what they wanted. Especially candy. She'd practiced tough love on both the parents and the children, but Frank was much older, a person of standing in his community. He probably wasn't used to being spoken to in such harsh terms. An alarming thought crossed Grace's mind. Maybe, by speaking out, she'd sabotaged the medical center. What would she say to Lucy?

Frank finally responded. "Is that so, little lady?"

Grace swallowed, compelled to tell him the truth. "I'm afraid it is. I'm very concerned that if you continue eating this sort of food and not exercise, one day you're going to wake up dead! And it'll be no one's fault but your own."

"I see," he said, eyeing the chicken in Grace's salad. "You're sounding like my wife. She's a real nag."

"Has it done any good?"

"'Course not! She's not a doctor. What would she know?"

So much for thinking Frank was a liberated man.

"She feeds me cardboard for breakfast and nothing tasty for dinner. I'm dying of food boredom!"

"Better that than of coronary artery disease," Grace snapped back, not in the least intimidated by his lamentations about his wife. "By cardboard, I assume you mean granola?"

Frank nodded.

"Unsweetened?"

"Yup."

"Do you have coffee for breakfast, as well?"

"Two cups. She won't let me have sugar or cream. She's thrown them out of the house."

"Good!"

"So I have extra when I get to the office."

Grace's shoulders slumped. "That's not how it works, Frank."

The poor man was still eyeing her chicken. Grace pushed her plate between them—the cruelest, unhealthiest thing to do to people trying to lose weight was to deprive them completely of food. "You may share my salad, Frank. And you and I are going to have a nice, long talk about your health, okay?"

She signaled the waiter to come and remove Frank's lunch. And the remainder of his beer. She then ordered a glass of water for him, since he didn't already have one.

Grace had never seen anyone look so dejected. "I'm sorry, Frank, but this is for your own good. What would Louella do without you?"

"My wife would have her turned into bacon."

Grace doubted that, but she knew Louella and Mrs. C. were not friends. "Then it's up to you to make sure that doesn't happen!" Grace leaned over the table, closer to Frank. "Are you willing to work with me on this?" she asked.

"Will I be hungry?"

"Not if I can help it. But you also won't be eating any artery-clogging crap, okay?"

Frank looked at her in a way that made Grace fear he'd refuse her advice. Finally, he nodded.

"Good!" she said. "First thing after lunch, I'm going to run a few tests on you."

"How you gonna do that?" he asked, smirking as if he had an excuse to delay the inevitable.

"I'm sure Lucy Cochrane would let me use her equipment at the maternity clinic."

"The maternity clinic! I'm not going there. It's full of pregnant women!"

Grace was unmoved. "No kidding. And most of them weigh far less than you do. So suck it up."

Frank had not only polished off the chicken in her salad, but also the lettuce and anchovies—Grace loved anchovies and now she was miffed she hadn't snaffled them for herself before deciding to share. She signaled for the check.

"What about dessert?" Frank asked, adding, "And I haven't told you all the stories about your aunt yet."

Grace knew he was stalling for time, stalling so she'd have to order more to eat for him, so she waved her hand, saying, "Your aunt Missy stories can wait for another day, we have more important things to tend to right now, like your health. Since they don't serve fruit salad here, we don't need dessert." She passed her credit card to the waiter. She got up and went to sign her credit card slip at the checkout counter, then turned and crooked her index finger at the mayor. "Come on, Frank. The rest of your life starts today."

GRACE CALLED LUCY and asked if she could use her facility to run a few tests. Lucy, of course, agreed, and on discovering Grace's patient was Frank, who didn't want to be seen surrounded by pregnant women, told Grace where to find the rear entrance.

Outside Rusty's, Frank opened the door of his enormous Cadillac for Grace. Once they were both inside, she said, "Frank, please don't tell me you drove your car all of two blocks from the town hall to Rusty's?"

His Caddy roared to life—more life than Grace feared Frank had left in him.

"'Course, I drive her everywhere. People need to know who's the boss around here. This old girl is a mark of the respect I'm given as mayor."

"Which you won't get if you're dead."

Frank had just pulled out onto Main Street. He slammed on his brakes, but fortunately there wasn't any other traffic.

"Now, look here, little lady. You gotta stop talkin' about me dyin', okay?"

"No, it isn't okay. If you have anywhere to go in town from now on, you're to walk. *Got it?*"

Frank's lips tightened and he pressed the accelerator, not taking his foot off it until they drove into the hospital's parking lot.

FRANK'S TEST RESULTS were worse than she'd expected. He was a hairsbreadth from a heart attack. She wanted to admit him right away, but true to form, Frank had resisted.

As they drove back to Spruce Lake, Grace called Mrs. C., asking her to close the shop and meet her and Frank in Grace's apartment. Neutral ground was best for news like this. She and Mrs. C. were going to stage an intervention. When they pulled into the parking lot, Jack was there with Millie.

Grace's dog just about twisted herself inside out with excitement to see her new owner. Grace felt much the same way about Millie. Already the dog had made a difference in her life. She'd given her a purpose—one she hadn't felt strongly in her busy Boston practice in too many months.

After effusive greetings between human and dog, Jack asked with concern, "What's up? I stopped by to find out how your meeting went when Mrs. C. got your call. Anything I can do? She's a bit of a mess. She knows you took him to the maternity clinic in Silver Springs. He isn't pregnant, is he?" he asked, and winked.

They both turned to look at Frank as he got out of his car—not without some difficulty. He had such a huge potbelly, he resembled a pregnant woman—one carrying octuplets.

Grace smiled, appreciating the attempt at levity. "No, I wish it was as simple as that. I need to talk to him and Mrs. C. Would you mind taking Millie for a while? I don't want an overexcited dog in the way."

Jack took Millie's leash. "Sure."

Grace glanced at the steps leading to her apartment and decided Frank probably wouldn't make it up them. But before she could stop him, Frank started up the stairs. He got about halfway, then halted, catching his breath. Mrs. C., who had been waiting by Grace's door, raced down to him. "Frank! What's the matter, you idiot?" she almost shrieked.

Grace turned to Jack. "Would you mind not taking Millie too far? I might need your help either to keep her from killing him or him from killing himself."

Jack leaned in and kissed Grace's cheek. The warmth of his lips, the touch of his hand as it cupped the back of her head, were just what she needed right now. "Call me and I'll be here in a nanosecond, okay?" he said.

Grace nodded, said, "Thanks," and began to mount the stairs to her apartment.

Frank was panting heavily, and Grace was having severe misgivings about the wisdom of making him climb those steps.

THANKFULLY, DURING THE drive from the hospital to Spruce Lake, Frank's usual ornery attitude seemed to have mellowed. Grace explained the tests she'd done, and Mrs. C.—who'd insisted she call her Edna—had tried saying, "I told you so!" more than once, but Grace had shushed her. The older woman had to understand that now wasn't the time for recriminations.

When she'd finished explaining how Frank's life-style had to change and change drastically, Edna had said, "Will you be Frank's doctor, Grace? I trust you. That old fool Jenkins has been pumping him full of prescription drugs for his heart, his liver, everything! And Frank thinks because he's got the drugs he can do whatever he wants."

Grace told them that, too often, people resorted to drugs, believing them to be the cure-all, a green light to continue destructive habits. Frank looked suitably chastened, if not terrified. Whether it was of his wife or his prognosis, Grace wasn't sure, but it was about time Frank took stock of his health and did something about it.

"I'm not a heart specialist," she said.

"I...I thought you knew what to do to help him," Edna said.

"I do. But I'd also like him to consult a cardiologist. In fact, if I can make an emergency appointment, I'd like him to see one in Denver tomorrow."

"Tomorrow! It's that bad?"

"The results aren't good. He needs to see a specialist."

Guessing that much of the alarm in Edna's expression was about entrusting her husband's health to a stranger, she said, "I'd be more than happy to look after Frank under the guidance of the cardiologist while I'm in Spruce Lake. Would that be all right?"

"Yes! Yes, please!" Edna grasped Grace's hand. "You're a godsend. I've been at my husband for ages. I put him on a diet, but I suspect he doesn't eat his salads and sneaks into Rusty's instead."

Grace smiled and stood. "I'll call some colleagues of mine in Boston and see if they can arrange anything with their colleagues in Denver. It might take a few hours. Why don't I stop by your place as soon as I have news?"

"That would be wonderful. Thank you so much, Grace!" Edna said.

Frank had got to his feet with difficulty and stood there wheezing. "Thanks, Doc," he said, and shuffled to the door. The poor man seemed to have aged ten years in the past hour or so. Grace felt guilty about it, but that was what she had to do to save his life—tell him the plain truth.

He turned to her at the door. "What am I allowed to have for dinner tonight?"

"Grilled chicken breast, no skin. As much salad as

you like with lemon juice for dressing. No dessert except a piece of fruit."

Frank looked totally miserable, while Edna looked triumphant that a doctor was now telling her husband what he could and couldn't eat.

"And don't drive your car home, Frank. You can manage the block from here to there, okay? Tomorrow morning, you and I are going to take a leisurely walk, the first of many."

Jack, waiting outside with Millie, bounded up the stairs and placed a hand under Frank's arm. Frank shrugged him off. "I ain't dead yet, boy!" he said, and took another step down.

"No one said you were, Frank, but I was taught to respect my elders, and since you're old and ornery, I'll help you down these stairs."

"Cheeky young whippersnapper," Grace heard Frank mumble as he allowed Jack to help him.

Grace leaned against her doorjamb, her arms crossed as she watched Edna and Frank cross the lot and walk down the back lane to their own house a block away.

Millie hobbled up the stairs, licked Grace's leg and wandered into the apartment. Jack followed her and stopped in front of Grace.

"Bad day?" he asked.

"Really bad. Hold me?"

They wrapped their arms around each other, Grace nestling her head against his strong chest and just breathing him in. Being with Jack was like being in a kind of sanctuary....

"Want to talk about it?"

Reluctantly Grace let him go and they went into her

apartment. She collapsed on the sofa beside Millie, who placed her nose on Grace's thigh, turning her sweet brown eyes up to Grace as if to say, "We've got each other, so everything will be fine now."

Grace hugged her dog, and then her shoulders began to tremble as she held back tears. Jack sat beside her, put his arm around her and said, "What's wrong? What can I do?"

"Everything's wrong! Frank is really ill and I'm worried I did the wrong thing by not admitting him to the hospital today. I should've called a cardiologist then and there instead of bringing him home!"

"So call a cardiologist now. Weren't you planning to do that, anyway? Set your mind at ease."

Grace looked up at him. "Thank you for being here— and being the voice of reason."

She got out her cell phone and called a cardiologist she knew in Boston. She told him about Frank's age and his test results.

Dr. Giles said, "Relax, Grace. You did the right thing. I doubt the patient would have allowed you to admit him, by the sound of it. Let me make a few inquiries. I'll have one of the best cardiologists in Denver call you, okay?"

Grace released a pent-up breath as she ended the conversation. "Thank God." She leaned her head against Jack.

"Feel like taking a walk to clear your head?" he asked. "I'd like to hear how the meeting went with the town today."

THE EVENING WALK ended up being just what Grace needed. She loved Jack's company and enjoyed walking as Millie met other dogs. During the walk, a cardiologist from Denver called and offered to squeeze Frank in the following day. She thanked him profusely and they changed direction toward Frank's house.

They were greeted on the front porch by his pet pig, Louella, who ignored Jack in favor of Grace and Millie. Satisfied that they weren't a threat to her esteemed position in Frank's life, she snorted and allowed them to pass.

Edna met them at the door. "Grace! Jack! Nice to see you both again so soon. Come in, please. Frank and I are just finishing dinner."

She showed them into the kitchen of their restored Victorian. Frank was sitting at the dinner table eyeing a sliced apple. He looked miserable. Grace guessed he would prefer brownies. Sitting next to him, she said, "I hope you liked your dinner, Frank. How are you feeling?"

"Hungry," he growled. "And now I get *this* for dessert!"

Grace stole one of the apple wedges and offered him another. He took it suspiciously.

"It won't bite," she assured him, and ate her own slice.

"Hey!" he said. "That's mine!"

"If you don't hurry up, I'll eat some more."

That motivated Frank to stop sulking and start eating.

"A cardiologist in Denver has cleared time in his schedule to see you tomorrow afternoon," she told the older couple. "I accepted the appointment on your behalf. I assume that's fine with you?"

"Thank you!" Edna cried. Frank was too busy chewing his apple to do anything other than nod.

"I don't have a car—otherwise, I'd drive you down myself," she said. "However, I'd like to attend the appointment, if you don't mind?"

"You'd do all that? For us? Now that's what I call being a *real* doctor!" Edna said. "But aren't there things you have to do here, Grace? Frank told me about the plans for the medical center. How exciting! I'm sure Missy would've loved to see her old home used in that way."

"I have a lot of paperwork to complete," Grace said. "But seeing Frank properly assessed and starting a course of treatment is more important right now."

Frank swallowed the last of his apple and said, "I can help you with the forms, little lady. And I do appreciate all your efforts today. My wife gave me quite a talking-to tonight." He placed his hand over Edna's.

"Old fool!" Edna muttered affectionately.

Grace and Jack exchanged smiles. Grace had been worried about Frank's agreeing to treatment, especially curtailing his diet or increasing his exercise, but she had a feeling that with her and Edna on his case, he had a chance.

Everyone agreed that Grace would meet them at the house at eleven the next morning to drive to Denver, and Jack and Grace waved goodbye, Millie pulling at her leash.

"I don't have much in the fridge to offer for dinner," Grace said. "But I could whip up a quiche and salad. That's pretty simple."

"Sounds great," Jack said. "I take it you're not up to going out tonight?"

Grace drew in a huge breath. "Thanks, but no. I'm drained and I'd like to work on the forms for a couple of hours before we leave for Denver in the morning."

Jack laid his palm against her cheek. "I could help with that, too."

"Thanks. But you have enough on your plate. Beth has those new plans for you to give us a quote on—I can see this costing a whole lot more than I'd budgeted for, but I think it's going to be worth it."

Just as soon as she'd got the approvals done and the work started and Frank established on a course of coronary care, she'd head back to Boston. She couldn't keep pretending she might stay in Spruce Lake. The daily emails from the clinic she shared with other specialists, asking when she expected to return, were making it harder and harder to resist the call of helping others. She'd just needed a break from medicine, to regroup. Well, she'd had that and now it was time to think about getting on with the rest of her life.

In spite of how Grace felt about him, she and Jack didn't have a future. There was too great a risk that he'd find out the truth. He'd hate her forever if he did, and that—more than the thought of moving halfway across the country and never seeing him again—was motivating her decision to leave Spruce Lake forever.

Chapter Eighteen

She'd miss this, Grace thought, the comfortable companionship she and Jack shared as they worked together in her tiny kitchen. He was not only easy on the eyes, he was easy company. Intelligent and with a keen sense of humor and social justice, he was everything she could want in a man. Yet she'd thrown all of that away thirteen years ago.

For a short while, she'd fantasized that they could "do over" their lives. But every time she got to the part where she decided to keep Amelia, everything went south. She could never envision being free of financial struggle and she'd seen too many marriages break down under that kind of financial strain. Grace had been poor growing up, and she didn't want that for her child, couldn't bear that her irresponsible actions had brought another child into the world who'd be denied opportunities. She'd lived that life herself, only escaping through the hard work that gained her a college scholarship. When she'd discovered she was pregnant she'd called her mother, who'd talked her into not telling Jack, begging her not to give up her dreams in order to marry him. When she'd asked if her mother regretted marrying her father, and having Grace, she'd said,

"What else would I do? I'm not qualified for anything. And besides that, I love your father. I belong with him. But you—get an abortion!"

After all these years, all the disappointments, Grace's mother still loved her father. Could she and Jack have ended up that way? Penniless but in love? It wasn't enough for Grace. It would never be enough.

She'd made the right decision in the end—for both her and their baby—but she still regretted it every day of her life. Strange how her mother had just assumed that Grace had taken her advice.

Jack leaned toward her and kissed her cheek, then went back to beating the custard for the quiche.

Grace mentally shook herself. She had to stop thinking about this. But the more time she spent with Jack, the more guilt she felt over her choice to give Amelia up and her failure to confess the truth to the baby's father.

"You're miles away. What's up?" he said, and poured the mix onto the premade pie crust Grace had set out. She placed the quiche in the oven, turned toward him, trying to distract him from further questions. She wrapped her arms around his neck. "Nothing," she said. "Want to make out?"

Jack's eyes glittered with arousal. "If you insist," he said, and lifted her onto the countertop.

GRACE'S PHONE RANG. As Jack blindly groped for it on the counter behind her, still kissing her neck, he knocked her wallet to the floor. He handed the phone to Grace and bent to retrieve the wallet, noticing that a photograph had fallen out. He picked it up and was about to slip it back inside, when he realized it was a photo of

Grace. She looked no older than she had when she'd graduated from high school, and she was holding a baby—a newborn, tightly bundled baby. He lifted the picture to eye level and his gaze collided with Grace's.

She was whiter than a ghost. "I'll call you back," she said, her fingers shaking as she switched off her phone.

"Who is this?" he asked.

The tears brimming in Grace's eyes terrified him. *"Who is this, Grace?"* he demanded.

She pressed her lips together and for a moment he was afraid she wouldn't answer him. He turned the photo over. On the back were the words *Amelia 6 lbs., 11 oz. May 25, 2000.*

He swallowed as he read the date and looked up at Grace again. Her lips were still tightly clamped but she could no longer hold back the tears. They welled from her eyes and streamed down her cheeks.

At last she said, "She's…our daughter."

Jack grasped the counter to steady himself. A thousand questions swirled through his mind, some more frightening than others. The worst was: if Grace had never mentioned her, did that mean she'd died?

He finally found his voice and asked, "Where is she?"

Grace slid off the countertop and reached out to him but he held the photograph firmly between them. "Where *is* she?" he demanded again. "What happened to her?"

"Jack…" she said, and faltered. "It's a long story."

"The short version will do," he snapped. "*Where* is my daughter?"

"I…gave her up for adoption."

Jack's knees almost buckled. The relief that his

daughter hadn't died was quickly replaced with anger so deep and bitter he could taste it. "You *what?*" he roared, barely able to keep control of his roiling emotions. Grace had given birth to their baby? *Grace had given their baby away?*

"I told you it was a long story," she said, moving toward him again. "Please. Let's sit down. I can explain everything."

Jack stepped back, feeling as if her touch would make this nightmare real.

"I don't want to hear any explanations. There's no forgiveness for what you've done," he said. "Tell me where my daughter is and I'll go and get her. That's all I want. I don't want you. I don't want your lies. I don't want you in my life! Just tell me where she is!"

Grace swiped at her tears, but Jack was so angry he was immune to them, immune to anything she might be suffering because what he was feeling was so much worse.

"I can't," she said, her voice breaking.

"*What?* You just gave our baby away to a pair of strangers? Did you walk up to someone on the streets of Boston and just hand her over?" He wanted to hurt her, the way she'd hurt him. "Or…or better yet, *sell* her?"

Grace's slap caught him unawares.

"How dare you!" she cried.

Jack gripped her arms. "No! How dare *you!* How dare you have our baby and not tell me! How dare you give her away! How dare you not let me have the opportunity to be part of her life. To be a father to her." He paced the tiny apartment, furious with Grace. "And you've been back here *how* long? Why didn't you tell me when I started work on the house? How could you have flirted with me for so long and kept this from me? You've been lying to me from the start!"

"If you'd let me explain—"

"No!" He cut her off. "There is no explanation that can justify this, Grace!"

"You were eighteen and halfway around the world—"

"Don't make this *my* fault!" Jack hissed. "*You* had my baby, you didn't tell me anything about it, then you gave her away!"

With all the shouting, Millie had gone to sit at Grace's feet. She looked at Jack, her head tilted as if trying to figure out what was going on.

He strode back to Grace, inches from her face, challenging her to look away, to hide her shame. "You have not only deprived me of knowing my daughter, you've deprived my parents of being grandparents to her, my brothers being uncles, her cousins from knowing her! Did you think about that even once, Grace? Did you think about anyone other than yourself in this whole scenario?"

When she didn't respond, he felt vindicated. He bent to scratch Millie's ear, letting her know he wasn't mad at her. He was rewarded with a warm lick. *At least one of the females in this room has a heart,* he thought bitterly.

"Your career was more important than our child, was that it?"

Without waiting for her answer, he stormed to the door, wrenched it open and looked back at her.

"I never want to see you again," he said and, with as much constraint as he could muster, went outside and slammed the door behind him.

Enraged at her betrayal, Jack stumbled down the steps, climbed into Betsy and thundered out of the parking area, his wheels spinning in the gravel.

Chapter Nineteen

Jack tore out of Spruce Lake, so blinded by rage that he didn't see the sheriff's department vehicle coming in the opposite direction. Before he could react and take his foot off the accelerator, the other truck's lights and siren were going and it made a U-turn to pursue him.

He pulled Betsy over and waited while it parked behind him. "Crap!" he muttered as he saw Matt jump out of the other vehicle and walk toward his car. He was tempted to make a break for it, while Matt was too far from his vehicle to give immediate chase—but Matt would catch him soon enough and then he'd really have some explaining to do. He didn't want Matt seeing him in this state, didn't want to admit why he was so upset. He needed time to digest everything he'd learned tonight and he couldn't do that with Matt interrogating him.

So he rolled down the window and said, "Just give me the ticket and save the lecture."

"Oh, you'll get the lecture, all right," Matt said, resting his hands on Betsy's window frame. "*And* the tick—" Matt halted midsentence and stuck his head inside to get a closer look at Jack. "What the hell happened to you?"

Jack scrubbed his eyes. "Dust."

"The hell it is! What's up, buddy?"

The concern in Matt's voice choked Jack up even more. "Nothing. I just need to be on my own."

Matt opened the door and started getting in. "Move over," he said, "we're taking a brotherly drive."

Jack knew there was no point in arguing with Matt. He was the most stubborn of the brothers.

"Let's go to Inspiration Point," Matt suggested.

"What? So we can neck?" Jack retorted.

"If you like," Matt said, and looked across at him.

Jack ignored his brother's teasing and stared through the windshield. No amount of gentle mockery could improve his mood.

Matt forgot to change gears as they rounded the bend toward Inspiration Point and cursed under his breath. "Stick shifts!" he muttered as he shoved Betsy into gear.

"Careful!" Jack warned. "She's not as young as she used to be."

Matt patted Betsy's dash in apology and said, "This is the longest relationship you've ever had with a woman."

Jack crossed his arms. "Well, it's over, so forget it."

"What? You and Betsy are calling it quits?" Matt said with a grin. "Apart from a brief flirtation with that floozy Al's driving now, you've been faithful to Betsy for how many years?" Matt changed down as the gradient up the hill to the Point increased. This time he was more gentle on Betsy. Gentle on the gears and gentle on the clutch.

"Grace had our baby and gave her up for adoption," Jack blurted.

"Whoa!" Matt cried as he nearly steered Betsy off the precipice. He fought the wheel and brought the old truck to a stop on the shoulder, cut the ignition and turned to Jack. "Run that by me again?"

"Grace had our baby, gave her up for adoption and never told me." Jack dug his knuckles into his eyes.

He felt Matt's hand on his shoulder, felt its warmth and strength.

"Tell me about it," Matt urged.

"Grace and I made love for the first and last time just before she left for college. The birth control must've failed. She got pregnant, didn't tell me and…because of her precious career aspirations, she gave our baby away."

Unable to stay in the truck with all his pent-up anger, Jack pushed open the door and got out, striding from Matt and Betsy.

It didn't take Matt long to catch up and pull Jack into a brotherly bear hug. Jack forced himself not to cling. He'd already shown enough weakness to his big brother; he couldn't let down his guard any further. "She had no intention of telling me any of this! I hate her! I didn't think I could hate anyone, but I do." He tried to pull out of the other man's embrace, but his brother held fast.

"Well, that's a relief to hear, buddy."

The comment surprised Jack. He'd been expecting Matt to defend Grace because that was what Matt did. He was the family protector. No wonder he'd become a cop!

Matt let go of him. "Because if you were indifferent, I'd be worried that there was no hope of salvaging this," his brother said. "You hate her at the moment, but deep down you really love her."

"I can do without your twisted pop psychology."

"Let's talk this out," Matt said, drawing Jack toward Betsy. He leaned against her and said, "Why didn't she tell you about the baby?"

"I don't know."

Matt nodded. "Then why did she give the baby up?"

"I don't know."

"Seems there's a lot you don't know about the circumstances, yet you're going off half-cocked and hating Grace."

"What part of 'Grace gave our baby up and didn't tell me' don't you understand?"

"Truthfully? Most of it. Grace is a good woman. There has to be a good reason. It's a pity you didn't bother hanging around to find out what it was."

When Jack remained silent, staring at the ground, struggling with his emotions, Matt said, "Let's go see her. Talk it out."

"No! I can't talk to her. I can't forgive her."

"Just as well you didn't take those final vows, Jack. You'd have made a lousy priest."

Jack's head snapped up at that. "Maybe so, but I'd like to think I'd have been a damned good father to my child."

FOR A GOOD FIVE MINUTES Grace stood stiffly, staring at the front door of her tiny apartment, hands clenched by her sides as she willed the tears not to fall. Jack's words played over and over in her brain. And then the tears came, tears she had no control over, tears she'd held inside for too long. They flowed down her cheeks as she gulped for air and grabbed for the tissues. How could she ever have thought of leaving this place? Of leaving

Jack? It wasn't until he'd stormed out of her life that she knew she needed him *in* her life.

Millie whined softly, and Grace sank to the floor and hugged her dog. "I've done something terrible, Millie, and I don't know how to make it right," she said, burying her face against Millie's soft fur.

Millie licked her as if that were the cure to all suffering. Grace half smiled and said, "What would I do without you, Millie?" That brought on a fresh bout of crying.

She'd messed up so badly but Grace knew that succumbing to self-pity wasn't going to help. If nothing else, she owed Jack an explanation, and since he wasn't ready to hear it in person she'd write to him. And then she was getting out of Spruce Lake—forever! She wiped her eyes and scrambled to her feet.

After washing her face, Grace returned the call she'd had to interrupt earlier.

Dr. Rivers accepted her apology for cutting him off and said, "I was calling to ask if we could move that appointment to 8:00 a.m. I know it's a lot to ask, but I've got an urgent meeting."

Grace knew how pressed good doctors were for time. "That's fine, Dr. Rivers," she assured him. "I'm just grateful you could fit Mr. Farquar in on such short notice."

"You're welcome. See you in the morning," he said.

Grace called the Farquars and told Edna about the change of plans. Far from finding it an inconvenience, the older woman said, "The sooner, the better, Grace. We'll stop by your place at six tomorrow. We'll need to leave early in case of traffic."

Hoping the other woman hadn't been aware of

Grace's teary voice before they hung up, Grace went into her bedroom and hauled out her suitcases. There was no point in staying here any longer. She'd continue to do what was needed to start the clinic because she'd made a commitment to Lucy, but as for staying and working in Spruce Lake—that just wasn't going to happen. She'd go back to Boston, pick up where she'd left off. And she was going to try to forget the man she loved.

Millie wandered into the room and looked at her curiously. "Want to come to Boston with me?" she asked.

Millie wagged her tail excitedly.

"I'll take that as a 'yes.' Come here." She held out her arms and Millie hopped over to her and let Grace hug her tightly. The dog's unconditional love tore at Grace's heart. She'd been so hell-bent on going to college, on becoming a doctor, amassing wealth, being the opposite of what her parents were, that she'd—

She'd lost sight of who *she* was.

Suitcases packed, Grace sat down at her tiny dining room table, where she'd shared such happy lunches and suppers with Jack, and wrote short notes to several people regarding her abrupt departure from Spruce Lake. The first was to Sally, apologizing for deserting her but promising to be available anytime she needed to talk about Aaron, or any of her children. Another to Lucy, explaining that while Lucy had her full support for the clinic, she'd be working remotely from Boston, doing the paperwork and submitting it online. The last note was to Edna Carmichael-Farquar. This was harder to write because she would have to deceive the elderly couple all morning. Tomorrow, she'd attend Frank's appointment and then afterward ask them to drop her at the airport, saying she needed to return to Boston immediately.

You're a coward! Grace admonished herself. She didn't have the guts to come clean to the Farquars to their faces. Instead, she wrote a check to cover the next three months' rent, then sealed it and the note in an envelope. That done, she set about writing a long letter to Jack.

It was hard to find the words at first, but in time she did and they flowed as profusely as her tears. It was well after midnight before she'd finished and placed the envelope containing Jack's letter beside the others. Tomorrow she'd tell Edna there was something for her on the table in the apartment.

Feeling emotionally drained, Grace stood under the shower, letting the tears flow once more.

TRUE TO HER WORD, Edna pulled up right at 6:00 a.m. Grace was waiting for them with her suitcases and Millie on her leash. She'd barely slept and had spent the past hour with ice packs on her eyes trying to lessen the telltale swelling that said she'd been crying most of the night.

But Grace was in control of her emotions now. She'd had a few hours to think and she'd made some firm decisions about her future—a future she hoped would eventually include Jack. But if not, it might include her daughter.

Taking a deep breath she got up from the bottom

step and went to say hello to the Farquars, towing one of the suitcases.

Frank began to get out of the passenger seat to help, but Grace said, "They're not heavy, I can manage."

She greeted Edna through the window and said, "I've had an emergency come up. Would you mind dropping me at the airport after Frank's appointment?"

"Sure thing. If it's an emergency, shouldn't we drop you first?" she asked, popping the trunk.

Grace loaded the first suitcase, which was light, because it only contained Millie's bed, food bowls and toys. She'd left a lot of her clothes boxed up in the apartment, with a note asking Edna to send them to Boston whenever it was convenient.

She hefted the second suitcase into the trunk and smiled at Edna. "I hope you don't mind if Millie comes with us?"

"Of course not, dear," Edna assured her. "But if you're just going for a short time, why not leave her here? She's welcome to stay with us."

"I...I'm not too sure how long I'll be. It could take a while." She shrugged. "It's a...family matter."

Edna nodded and said, "I see. Well, if there's anything you need me to do while you're gone, just ask."

Grace couldn't believe she was walking away from good people like Edna Carmichael and all the friends she'd made in Spruce Lake over the past couple of weeks. But she had her penance to pay, and until she'd done that, she could never look these people in the eye again.

FRANK'S APPOINTMENT WENT well. Dr. Rivers was thorough and backed up the diet plan Grace had outlined, which delighted Edna no end and left Frank sulking. However, with a male doctor supporting the women, Frank had no choice but to pay attention to his health. Dr. Rivers prescribed some medication and made an appointment to follow up on Frank's progress in two weeks.

Frank seemed in better spirits by the time they all piled into the Caddy to drive to the airport. He was especially relieved that he wasn't facing surgery. However, Dr. Rivers had told him that if he didn't watch his diet and general health, he could be. Within the year!

Millie greeted them effusively. She'd had to be locked in the car during the appointment, but fortunately the garage was under the building, so she was cool in the shade, and with the Caddy's windows rolled down a little, she had sufficient air. She'd probably slept the whole time they'd been gone.

AN HOUR LATER, Millie was being loaded into the crate Grace had purchased at a Denver pet store in preparation for her very first flight.

Grace had nearly burst into tears as she'd said her farewells to the Farquars at the airport curb, insisting they get on their way to Spruce Lake rather than come in and wait with her.

At Boston's Logan Airport, Millie and Grace were reunited amid much happy tail-wagging and many wet kisses. Fortunately, she found a cab that would accept a dog—something Grace hadn't considered the night before when she'd decided to take Millie to Boston.

Letting herself into her apartment overlooking the harbor, she was hit by a blast of hot, stuffy air because the place had been locked up for several weeks. Millie bounded inside to look out the fifth-floor windows. Grace switched on the air conditioner and unpacked Millie's suitcase, placing her bed beside the sofa and filling her water and food bowls. Then, exhausted, she collapsed onto her sofa and stretched out, the only sound in the room Millie snuffling her kibble. Starving, Grace realized she hadn't eaten since yesterday at lunch— she'd been too stressed to eat the meal she and Jack had prepared and she'd skipped breakfast and lunch today, apart from a pack of pretzels on the plane. She called her favorite Chinese restaurant and ordered takeout, then went into her study and searched through the filing cabinet. At the very back, tucked underneath the vertical files, she found what she was looking for.

Returning to the living room, Grace shuffled through the papers until she located the phone number she needed. She had to do this now, not tomorrow, not next week.

With trembling fingers, she punched in the number and waited.

"Amelia Johansen speaking."

Grace froze. She hadn't given a thought to the fact that her daughter might answer the phone.

"Hello?"

Oh, God! What should she do? Hang up? No! This was her daughter. She couldn't hang up on her.

Grace cleared her throat. "Hi! This is Gr— Dr. Saunders," she said. "Could I speak with your mom or dad, please?"

"Sure," Amelia said, and Grace's heart turned over at

the sound of her daughter's voice. "Mom! Dad! There's some doctor on the phone for you!"

Grace heard the phone being put down and Amelia— her child—walking away, humming. She smiled at that. She used to hum to herself. What did her daughter look like? Grace wondered. Was she tall, dark-haired, blue-eyed like her father? For twelve long years, Grace had resisted learning anything about her, fearing that if she did, she'd want to go and claim her in a weak moment— which was, of course, totally illegal under the terms of the adoption. But still, she didn't trust herself, so she'd asked Amy and Gil Johansen not to send her photos or updates on Amelia, although she did make sure it was okay for her to send presents on Amelia's birthdays and at Christmas. She signed the cards *Grace,* not *Mom.* Amy was Amelia's mom.

"Hello?"

Grace recognized Amy's voice. Even after all these years, she sounded the same.

"Amy, it's Grace Saunders," she said quickly. "Don't worry, I didn't tell Amelia who I am."

"Thank God!" Amy breathed. "She said it was a doctor on the phone."

"I *am* a doctor, Amy."

"Oh." She could tell the other woman was confused, imagined her taking a seat, trying to deal with the fact that her daughter's birth mother was calling after all these years.

"What can I do for you, Gr—er, Doctor?" she asked, and Grace guessed Amelia had come back into the room. "Can you give me a moment?" Amy asked. "I need to go somewhere more private."

"What's up, Mom?" Grace heard her daughter ask. "Gramma's okay, isn't she?"

Her daughter sounded concerned—so Amelia was a caring person. That was good. Better than good. It meant the Johansens were raising her properly.

"Gramma's fine, honey. I just didn't want to interrupt your reading."

And her daughter liked to read? Grace felt her heart swell. More than ever, she wanted to meet this little girl.

"Okay, I'm in another room. What can I do for you, Grace?" she asked again.

Grace took a deep breath, unsure how her request would be received. "Remember, when you adopted Amelia, that I had one request?"

"Ye-es," the other woman said. "You asked if you could meet her, when you felt it was time."

"It's time," Grace said, and her voice broke. She grabbed at the bridge of her nose, trying to stem her tears.

"Grace? Are you all right?" Amy asked. "Are you crying?"

"I am," Grace admitted, half laughing at herself. "I am. But they're happy tears, I think."

"That's good," the other woman said.

Amy was so calm. It was one of the things that had helped Grace choose the Johansens to be Amelia's parents. She wanted her to have a mother who was calm, who wouldn't fly off the handle or be impatient. A mother who would love her unconditionally.

Guilt pierced Grace's heart. Her request might drive a wedge between Amy and Amelia. She couldn't do that to them. "Forget it," she said quickly. "Forget I called."

She was about to hang up when she heard Amy say loudly, "Grace!"

Amy was usually soft-spoken, but her shout made Grace lift the phone to her ear again. "I'm still here," she said.

"Thank goodness! I've wanted to get in touch with you for a while. She wants to meet you, Grace!" Amy spoke almost breathlessly. "Ever since her last birthday, she's been pestering me with questions about you. It's so strange, because before that she hardly ever did. Please say you still want to meet her, too?"

Grace could have wept with joy. "Thank you!" she breathed.

"Don't thank me, thank *you,* Grace, for giving us the gift of our beautiful daughter."

Grace closed her eyes, knowing she *had* done the right thing by giving Amelia to these kind and loving parents. But she'd done the wrong thing by denying Amelia's father knowledge of her—and she needed to make that right.

"I'd like to arrange to meet Amelia as soon as possible, Amy. But first I need to tell you something. And you might not like it."

HALF AN HOUR LATER, Grace hung up the phone. How different she felt from last night, when she thought her world had ended. Tomorrow, she would meet her daughter. Elation bubbled up inside Grace, spilling over until she laughed out loud. And not just meet her, she was going to spend the weekend with Amelia and her family. Amy had invited her to stay so they could all get to know one another.

Amy wasn't upset that Grace had lied about Amelia's father when they'd signed the adoption paperwork. The biological father had to agree to the adoption, so Grace had stated "Father Unknown" on Amelia's birth certificate. In fact, Amy had wanted to hear all about Jack, what he did, where he lived. Grace had told her everything—about how they'd met and eventually split up, Jack's service with the peace corps, his time in the seminary, his apprenticeship program for disadvantaged youth. She'd spoken with pride of his achievements so Amy would know what a good person Amelia's biological father was.

From Amy, she'd learned that Amelia dreamed of becoming a doctor, that she read profusely, played lacrosse and had a lot of friends.

"I'm going to meet my daughter tomorrow!" she told Millie, and rubbed her ears. Millie wagged her tail and licked Grace's hand. "And you've been invited along to meet her, too!" Millie's tail wagged harder.

In her bedroom Grace searched through her wardrobe, looking for something suitable to wear the next day. Everything seemed too formal and Amy had told her to dress casual. But the only really casual clothes Grace had were those in her suitcase or back in Spruce Lake. She rushed out to the living room and rummaged around until she came up with her denim skirts. "Perfect!" she said, taking the longer of the two skirts to her laundry room.

Once the skirt was washed and pressed, Grace laid out her clothes for the following day—a white camisole, a three-quarter-sleeve blouse she could leave open overtop, designer sandals. After all, she needed to show off that pedicure. Packing a few items in an overnight bag, Grace had to take a deep breath. She was almost jumping out of her skin with joy and anticipation.

Her takeout had arrived while she was talking with Amy. Grace reheated it and curled up on the sofa, eating her kung pao chicken right out of the container with chopsticks while she watched her favorite Sandra Bullock movie.

And then she was being awakened by the insistent buzzing of her cell phone. Grace sat up groggily, realizing she'd fallen asleep in front of the television. She glanced at the screen. Jack.

Grace couldn't talk to him right now. First, she'd meet her daughter, then she'd deal with Jack. She switched off her cell, stumbled to the bathroom, showered and fell asleep still wrapped in her towel.

Chapter Twenty

Jack cursed and slammed his cell phone down on the countertop.

"I'm so sorry, dear," Mrs. C. told him as they stood in the tiny kitchen of the apartment over her shop. "I didn't find the letters until just now. Frank and I spent the day in Denver and didn't get home till late. Then I cooked his dinner and it was only afterward that I remembered Grace saying she'd left something here for me. I didn't realize there was a whole pile of letters for various people."

"It's okay, Mrs. C. I'm just grateful you didn't wait till morning to let me know."

"Would you like me to try calling her?"

"No point. Her phone's going straight to voice mail and I have no other way of contacting her."

"Would she be in the Boston phone directory?"

"No, she told me she has an unlisted number."

"That's a shame. What else can we do?"

Jack liked that Mrs. C. wanted to make it her mission to get ahold of Grace. Lucky he'd still been in town when the old lady called to tell him Grace had left him a letter. He'd almost not come, he was so angry with her. But it had chilled him to the bone when Mrs. C.

confessed that Grace had paid three months' rent—and asked to have the rest of her belongings sent on to Boston. Jack then knew Grace had left with no intention of returning. He *had* to know what the letter to him said.

He'd read it, not missing the tearstains and her brutal honesty about why she hadn't told him about their child, why she'd given her up. And because Grace had provided Mrs. C. with her shipping address, he now knew where to find her.

"You, my dear Mrs. C., are going home to look after that husband of yours. And I'm going to find Grace!"

The old woman's face lit up and she clapped her hands. "How romantic!" she said breathlessly.

"I'm going to Boston to get my lady back. And find our daughter."

Once he'd left, Jack called two different airlines and found a flight leaving at midnight from Denver and arriving in Boston via Newark around eight in the morning. He didn't have time to go home and pack anything; he needed to hotfoot it to Denver to catch his flight. The sooner he got to Grace, the better. The sooner he told her what a complete horse's backside he was and beg for her forgiveness, the better.

GRACE WOKE EARLY, thrilled to be meeting her daughter. Amy had invited her for lunch, but when Grace was going through her mail, killing time before she left, Amy called, saying Amelia was so excited she'd asked if Grace could come sooner.

"I'm on my way!" Grace said, leaping up from the sofa, scattering the mail in her haste. She ran the brush through her hair one final time, grabbed Millie's leash

and the overnight bag and raced out her front door—
slap-bang into Jack's broad chest.

"Hey!" he said. "Where are you off to in such a
hurry?"

Grace just stared at him mutely.

Jack? Jack was here in Boston? In her apartment?

Maybe she'd dreamed that phone call this morning
and was still asleep? No, it wasn't a dream, Millie was
going insane at the sight of him.

"Gracie?"

His use of her old nickname snapped Grace out of
her trance and she shook her head, unable to grasp that
he was really here. "How…how did you find me?" she
asked.

"You left your address for Mrs. C., remember?"

"Oh, yeah." Grace couldn't think of an intelligent
thing to say.

"So. Where are you going?" he asked again, indicating her overnight bag.

"Why are you here?" she countered, not ready to tell
him were she was headed.

"I got your note and tried to call you, but your phone
was off. So I decided to fly here and talk to you in person."

"In person?"

He frowned. "Yes, in person. Look, can we go inside?" he said, trying to move her backward into the
apartment, but Grace held her ground.

"No!" she said, still having trouble with this surreal
situation. Never in a million years had she imagined
finding Jack on her doorstep. "I have an appointment.
I have to leave."

"Can it wait? I have something important I need to say to you."

"I think you said it all yesterday, Jack. I understand. You hate me." She could feel the tears again, and she needed to get out of there before she lost her composure. "Goodbye," she said, and pushed past him toward the elevators.

He caught her arm as she pressed the down button.

"Grace, please? Give me five minutes?"

Grace's shoulders sagged. Since he'd bothered to fly all this way, she could do that, even if it was to listen to more abuse about the fact that she'd hidden the existence of their child from him. She deserved it and owed him at least five minutes for what she'd done. "Okay." She led the way back to her apartment. Millie paused on the threshold, unsure what was happening. "Come, girl!" she said, slapping her thigh.

Leaving her overnight bag by the door, Grace went to the wall of windows that looked out over the harbor. It was a calming view, in spite of all the harbor traffic. She needed to work on being calm. Crossing her arms, as if to protect herself, she waited.

"I've been a complete horse's ass," Jack said.

She turned toward him, and he held up his hand. "Don't say anything—just hear me out, okay?"

FIVE MINUTES LATER, true to his word, Jack stopped speaking. It was the longest speech she'd ever heard him make, but it was heartfelt and full of apology. *He* was asking her to forgive *him?*

Unable to speak, she held out a hand to him. Jack crossed the room and pulled her into his arms. "I can't live without you, I don't want to live without you. Please forgive me, Grace. If you'll come back to Spruce Lake with me, I'll never mention our child again. It'll kill me not to know her, but you mean everything to me. And if that's the trade-off, then I can deal with it."

Grace lifted a hand to his cheek and said, "I was about to go and *meet* our daughter when you arrived. Would you like to come, too?"

This time Jack was mute, so she said, "Her name is Amelia Johansen and she lives on Cape Cod with her parents, Amy and Gil. They've invited me to stay for the weekend so Amelia and I can get to know each other. I'm sure they'd all want to meet you. Especially Amelia."

Tears brimmed in Jack's eyes as he hugged her. "Yes," he said. "Yes, yes, yes!"

As THEY PULLED into the driveway of the neatly tended Cape Cod home, the front door swung open and a young teen appeared on the doorstep.

"Is that her?" Jack asked, his voice choked with emotion.

"She looks the right age," Grace said.

"She looks like you."

He said the words so softly she turned to him and saw his smile—the Jack smile she loved so much. "Shall we go and meet her?" she asked, barely able to keep from wrenching her door off its hinges as they got out.

Millie was pacing the backseat, sensing excitement in the air. She gave a woof at the same time that a Jack Russell terrier shot out the front door of the house and dashed toward them. He barked furiously, protecting his home against the intruders.

Then Millie jumped out, landing gracefully on her three legs, and he went crazy. Barking and leaping before detecting she wasn't a threat, he sniffed her diligently, then came to greet Grace and Jack.

The teen had made her way to their little group. Jack was ruffling the terrier's ears but then straightened. "What's his name?" he asked the girl as a way of breaking the ice.

"Jack," she said, then, as if realizing the coincidence, laughed.

Jack was nearly knocked off his feet. She was almost the image of Gracie when she laughed. A wide, open smile, shiny light brown hair and…blue eyes! So she had his eyes. Cool!

He held out his hand. "You must be Amelia. I'm Jack. And this," he said, pulling Grace to his side—since she seemed to have lost all ability to speak, "is Grace."

"Hi," the girl said shyly as she shook their hands. To cover her shyness, she dropped to the ground and petted Millie. Jack the Jack Russell, in a fit of jealousy, threw himself into her lap, wedging himself between Amelia and the canine intruder. Amelia giggled, serving to relieve Grace's nervousness about meeting her daughter after all these years.

Amelia got to her feet and said, "Come on in. Mom's been dying to see you."

At that moment an older woman, her hair graying slightly at the temples, came down from the doorstep and walked toward them, wiping her hands on her apron.

Amy! Grace thought. The uterine cancer survivor

who wasn't able to bear children. She'd promised Grace she'd take good care of her child, love her, teach her right from wrong.

Amy enfolded Grace in a warm hug, holding her tight. The other woman might have twenty years on Grace but she was strong. Grace hugged her back, saying, "It's so good to see you, Amy."

Amy eventually released her and stood back, studying Grace. "You haven't changed a bit, Grace. Still as beautiful as ever. And our daughter takes after you!"

She turned to scrutinize Jack and said, "Except she has her father's eyes. I'm delighted to meet you." And before Jack could shake her hand, she pulled him into a hug, as well.

Grace was pleased to see that he returned the embrace with equal gusto. For one awful moment during the drive here, she'd wondered if she'd done the right thing, asking Jack along. What if he'd demanded custody of his daughter, tried to tear her away from these good people and the only home she knew?

Legally, Jack could claim her, since he'd never signed the papers relinquishing Amelia. But he'd guessed Grace's thoughts and assured her that if he was happy with the people who'd adopted Amelia, he wouldn't make a fuss. Grace crossed her fingers and prayed that the Johansens would live up to his expectations.

"What's all this?" Grace heard someone say, and pivoted toward the cop car that had pulled into the driveway behind them. Gil Johansen was climbing out, dressed in his uniform, looking much the same as he had the day Grace first met him and decided she'd like a small-town cop to be her daughter's father. He'd gained a few pounds over the years but still had that gorgeous smile, those kind, dark eyes.

"Gil!" she said, greeting him with a kiss on the cheek that turned into a bear hug from him.

Introductions were made all around again and Gil said, "So what do you think of our little girl?" as he drew Amelia to his side.

The girl rested her arm around her father's waist, looking happy and at home there.

"She's beautiful!" Grace breathed, taking another long look at her daughter.

"She's the image of her mom at that age," Jack said.

"You've known Grace that long?" Amelia asked, and Grace wondered if she detected hurt in her daughter's voice.

"Almost," Jack said, glancing at Grace. "I met your mom…I mean *Grace,* when we were both sixteen."

"It's okay," she said. "I don't mind you saying Grace is my mom, because she is and so is my mom!" She laughed and it broke the tension. She held out her free hand and Jack took it, walking into the house with her two fathers. Her two mothers watched them with tears in their eyes.

"You've done a wonderful job of raising her, Amy," Grace said. "She's a remarkable young lady."

Amy laughed and put her arm around Grace as they, too, walked toward the house. "She's not always an angel," Amy warned. "Especially since she hit puberty. But thank you. We're both very proud of our little girl and love her to pieces. Now come on inside. I've baked lemon drizzle cake. It's Gil's and Amelia's favorite and they're hoping it'll be yours, too."

THE DAY COULDN'T have been better. Before lunch they all took a walk along the nearby beach, the dogs chasing each other and any object thrown remotely near them.

They then enjoyed lunch on the large veranda overlooking the Johansens' backyard, which was filled with flowers and well-established trees.

That evening, Jack treated them all at a local seafood restaurant on the waterfront. It was the perfect ending to a perfect day, with their perfectly happy daughter and her parents.

Grace hadn't pointed out that she and Jack weren't in a relationship when Amy showed her to the guest room, so that night she and Jack shared the king-size bed, usually reserved for Amelia's grandparents.

Lulled by the sound of the distant surf, for the first time in too long Grace slept like a baby, right where she wanted to be—wrapped in Jack's strong arms.

Epilogue

Jack and Grace got married that fall in the Johansens' backyard. The entire O'Malley clan flew out for the simple ceremony, since Amelia's adoptive grandparents were too elderly to fly.

The garden had rung with the excited shouts of children and the barking of two very happy dogs. Edna and Frank had also made the trip. Frank, fifty pounds lighter, looked fitter than anyone could remember. He left Louella back home in Spruce Lake—much to everyone's relief.

Sarah and Mac O'Malley had cherished meeting another grandchild, and although distance prevented Amelia from being an everyday visitor to Two Elk, she'd already been to the ranch twice—once with Amy and Gil and the second time on her own. She'd fit right in, learned to ride and gotten along famously with all of her cousins.

Sarah was delighted that her granddaughter had inherited Jack's and her blue eyes. They'd developed a close rapport, and every evening of Amelia's visits she and Sarah could be found on the back porch, knitting blankets for charity or sewing quilts to be sold in the thrift store in town to benefit animal rescue.

The clinic had been completed and opened on September 1, Aunt Missy's birthday. The ribbon-cutting ceremony was attended by people from all over the county, including many of the old-timer miners who regaled everyone with tales of Missy's school days. The renovations turned up a number of photographs of the old house and Missy and scenes of the town taken in the 1920s. Jack had them copied and the originals framed and hung in the Medical Center as a tribute to Aunt Missy. Grace was delighted.

Grace worked at the clinic full-time as a family practitioner, but was hoping to lighten her load once two more physicians started in the new year.

It was mid-December and Jack and Grace were preparing their home because Amelia was spending part of the Christmas holidays with them. Amelia had declared the cabin one of her favorite places in the whole world, and she was fine with sleeping on the sofa for a few nights. So it was decided she'd spend a couple of days with Grace and Jack, and the rest of her holiday with Grandma Sarah and Grandpa Mac and Luke's family at Two Elk.

As she watched Millie snoozing in her dog bed in front of the fire, happiness filled Grace's heart. Jack was trimming the tree, taking more care than Grace felt necessary—Christmas trees were Christmas trees. They were all beautiful in their own way, and their eight-foot monster was more than spectacular, even without the decorations. Unable to resist, she grabbed the front of Jack's shirt as he passed her and pulled him down onto the sofa.

He lifted her onto his lap and said, "What's up, lazy-bones? We've still got a tree to decorate."

"I was advised not to overdo it. To put my feet up whenever I get the chance."

Jack nuzzled her neck. "Hmm." He sighed against her throat. "Who by?"

"Lucy."

Jack sat up and looked at her, eyes narrowed. "Lucy your friend? Or Lucy the OB/GYN?"

"Lucy the latter."

"You're kidding." A smile as wide as Colorado broke across his face.

Grace touched her finger to his lips and he drew it into his mouth.

"I think your doing something along these lines got me into this state in the first place," she teased.

He let go of her finger and said, "You're sure? About the baby?"

"Absolutely. I wanted you to be the first to know."

"Thank you," he said, his voice gravelly with emotion. "Can I ask you a question?"

"Anything."

"Can we make Amelia the second person to know? Since this will be her little brother or sister."

"Of course. Should we call her now?"

Jack touched her hand. "Let's tell her in person. She'll be here in a couple of days. Can you keep a secret that long?"

"Hey, I'm the queen of keeping secrets," she said. "I kept the biggest secret in the world from you for nearly thirteen years. Remember?"

Jack grinned. All was forgiven, so there was no

heartache when they discussed Amelia and her adoption. They'd both agreed the Johansens were the perfect adoptive parents for their daughter. She was a contented child who wanted for nothing and had all the love in the world to give.

"I remember," Jack said, then turned playful as he growled, "Come here, wife!" and lunged for her.

Amid squeals and giggles, Grace allowed Jack to carry her to their bedroom and place her on the bed. He knelt over her, kissing her deeply. Then he kissed her abdomen, where their child resided.

"I love you, Grace. I always have. And I always will," he said. He gently undressed his wife and made love to her, the way a man should make love to a woman.

The way Grace had dreamed of all those years... only better!

* * * * *

REQUEST YOUR FREE BOOKS!

2 FREE NOVELS PLUS 2 FREE GIFTS!

LOVE, HOME & HAPPINESS

YES! Please send me 2 FREE Harlequin® American Romance® novels and my 2 FREE gifts (gifts are worth about $10). After receiving them, if I don't wish to receive any more books, I can return the shipping statement marked "cancel." If I don't cancel, I will receive 4 brand-new novels every month and be billed just $4.49 per book in the U.S. or $5.24 per book in Canada. That's a savings of at least 14% off the cover price! It's quite a bargain! Shipping and handling is just 50¢ per book in the U.S. and 75¢ per book in Canada.* I understand that accepting the 2 free books and gifts places me under no obligation to buy anything. I can always return a shipment and cancel at any time. Even if I never buy another book, the two free books and gifts are mine to keep forever.

154/354 HDN FVPK

Name   (PLEASE PRINT)

Address   Apt. #

City   State/Prov.   Zip/Postal Code

Signature (if under 18, a parent or guardian must sign)

Mail to the **Harlequin® Reader Service:**
IN U.S.A.: P.O. Box 1867, Buffalo, NY 14240-1867
IN CANADA: P.O. Box 609, Fort Erie, Ontario L2A 5X3

Want to try two free books from another line?
Call 1-800-873-8635 or visit www.ReaderService.com.

* Terms and prices subject to change without notice. Prices do not include applicable taxes. Sales tax applicable in N.Y. Canadian residents will be charged applicable taxes. Offer not valid in Quebec. This offer is limited to one order per household. Not valid for current subscribers to Harlequin American Romance books. All orders subject to credit approval. Credit or debit balances in a customer's account(s) may be offset by any other outstanding balance owed by or to the customer. Please allow 4 to 6 weeks for delivery. Offer available while quantities last.

Your Privacy—The Harlequin® Reader Service is committed to protecting your privacy. Our Privacy Policy is available online at www.ReaderService.com or upon request from the Harlequin Reader Service.

We make a portion of our mailing list available to reputable third parties that offer products we believe may interest you. If you prefer that we not exchange your name with third parties, or if you wish to clarify or modify your communication preferences, please visit us at www.ReaderService.com/consumerschoice or write to us at Harlequin Reader Service Preference Service, P.O. Box 9062, Buffalo, NY 14269. Include your complete name and address.

Welcome back to MUSTANG VALLEY,
*and Cathy McDavid's final book in this series.
Conner Durham has gone from flashy executive to simple
cowboy seemingly overnight. At least Dallas Sorrenson
has appeared back in his life—and she's
apparently single!*

The laughter, light and musical, struck a too-familiar chord. His steps faltered, and then stopped altogether. It couldn't be her! He must be mistaken.

Conner's hands involuntarily clenched. Gavin wouldn't blindside him like this. He'd assured Conner weeks ago that Dallas Sorrenson had declined their request to work on the book about Prince due to a schedule conflict. Her wedding, Conner had assumed.

And, yet, there was no mistaking that laughter, which drifted again through the closed office door.

With an arm that suddenly weighed a hundred pounds, he grasped the knob, pushed the door open and entered the office.

Dallas turned immediately and greeted him with a huge smile. The kind of bright, sexy smile that had most men— Conner included—angling for the chance to get near her.

Except, she was married, or soon to be married. He couldn't remember the date.

And her husband, or husband-to-be, was Conner's former coworker and pal. The man whose life remained perfect while Conner's took a nosedive.

"It's so good to see you again!" Dallas came toward him.

He reached out his hand to shake hers. "Hey, Dallas."

With an easy grace, she ignored his hand and wound her arms loosely around his neck for a friendly hug. Against his better judgment, Conner folded her in his embrace and drew her close. She smelled like spring flowers and felt like every man's fantasy. Then again, she always had.

"How have you been?"

Rather than state the obvious, that he was still looking for a job and just managing to survive, he answered, "Fine. How 'bout yourself?"

"Great."

She looked as happy as she sounded. Married life obviously agreed with her. "And how is Richard?"

"Actually, I wouldn't know." An indefinable emotion flickered in her eyes. "As of two months ago, we're no longer engaged."

It took several seconds for her words to register; longer for their implication to sink in.

Dallas Sorrenson was not just single, she was available.

Look for COWBOY FOR KEEPS, coming this March 2013 only from Harlequin American Romance!

HAREXP0313